ELISSA'S ODYSSEY

PHOENIX RISING
2

ELISSA'S ODYSSEY

ERICA VERRILLO

Random House New York

Text copyright © 2008 by Erica Verrillo
Map copyright © 2008 by Omar Rayyan

All rights reserved.
Published in the United States by Random House Children's Books, a division of Random House, Inc., New York.

Random House and colophon are registered trademarks of Random House, Inc.

Visit us on the Web! www.randomhouse.com/kids

Educators and librarians, for a variety of teaching tools, visit us at
www.randomhouse.com/teachers

Library of Congress Cataloging-in-Publication Data
Verrillo, Erica F.
Elissa's odyssey / Erica Verrillo. — 1st ed.
p.   cm. — (Phoenix rising trilogy ; bk. 2])
Summary: On their way home after defeating the Khan, Elissa becomes separated from her donkey, Gertrude, and friend Maya, so with the hope of being reunited, she hitches a ride with the unusual crew aboard the precarious Swamp Maiden.
ISBN: 978-0-375-83948-1 (trade) — ISBN: 978-0-375-93948-8 (lib. bdg.) —
ISBN: 978-0-375-83949-8 (pbk.)
[1. Human-animal communication—Fiction. 2. Human-plant relationships—Fiction.
3. Magic—Fiction. 4. Fantasy.] I. Title.
PZ7.V61315Ej 2008
[Fic]—dc22
2007022944

Printed in the United States of America

10 9 8 7 6 5 4 3 2 1

First Edition

For my daughter, Maya

Contents

ELISSA'S ODYSSEY

Prologue

The Ancient One sat before her hearth, waiting. It had been eight months since she had sent the Seeker into the world. The Ancient One threw another log on the fire, measuring with her eyes the length of time it took to turn the brown tree flesh into white bone. As she watched the flames devour the wood, she counted silently: *One, two, three, four, five.* She did not know, or care, what she was counting—minutes, months, miles. What did measurements matter if one was *cold*?

What is taking her so long? she wondered. *I haven't got all millennium.*

She jabbed her crooked stick impatiently into the fire.

"Here!" she said, dredging the stick through

the tiny mountains and valleys of glowing cinders. "Go here, and here!"

But even as she mapped the long, meandering route—southward and then eastward—it was covered under a desert of shifting ash.

The Ancient One shook her head. "You'll go where I tell you to go," she muttered. And with a patience born of desperation, she traced the Seeker's path again . . . and again, and again.

Welcome to Alhamazar

Some say the world is flat, like a plate, while others insist the world is round, like a bean pot. However, as all properly educated people know, the world is actually shaped like a bowl, gently sloping downward and inward, cupping the land and sea securely within its edges. At the far northern rim of this bowl lies a ring of mountains so high that no human being has ever scaled them. These mountains hold up the sky, preventing it from falling down and crushing the earth. All the lands in which people dwell are beautiful, from the tiniest forest glade to the loftiest mountain, for any land that provides a home is lovely to the eye—with the possible exception of the Great Desert.

Those who have never lived among its shifting

sands say that the Great Desert has a face only a mother could love. Pocked, pitted, strewn with boulders, creased with barren gullies and ravines, bruised by the hot sun, and scarred by fierce sandstorms, the desert is a land loved by few and feared by many. But those who do love the ugliest of Nature's faces do so with all their hearts. They are known as the Blue People, a people whose spirits are as vast and unyielding as the desert they defend, for, like the desert, they cannot be conquered.

Anyone choosing to cross the desert may do so only with the permission, and usually in the company, of the Blue People. To attempt such a journey alone is to risk a slow, agonizing death, as the desert likes to hide its life-giving waters from strangers. The other risks—being captured by slave traders or bitten by poisonous snakes—pale in comparison to death by thirst. The Blue men are unsurpassed as guides and invincible as warriors, for life in the desert is harsh and a knowledge of where and how to strike is as useful for a Blue man as it is for a cobra. Most people prefer to avoid both.

Elissa was not in a position to avoid either.

The Blue People were leading her and Maya to safety, and the snakes liked to cuddle up with her at night. Being chased across the desert, bombarded by sandstorms, nearly dying of thirst, and having to confront the Khan single-handedly—not to mention his army—was far more trying than this relatively dull journey to Alhamazar. Nevertheless, after weeks of eating sand, shaking affectionate reptiles out of her boots, and being jostled around on top of Ralph's swaying hump, Maya and Elissa were both ready for a change. Even more so Gertrude, who, in the absence of fresh pasture, had lapsed into a determined, sullen silence. The miserable donkey hardly gave Ralph a twitch of her tail in spite of the camel's many hopeful, but completely futile, attempts to lure her into conversation.

"How much farther?" Elissa had not meant to ask the question aloud, but Ralph, with his sharp ears, had heard her. The camel craned his neck around and turned his gorgeous eyes to Elissa.

"We are not far from our destination," he said. "Are you ladies sufficiently comfortable? Would you like me to halt?"

Elissa answered quickly, before Ralph could

offer them a picnic, a brisk walk, a game of cards, some tea. "No, don't stop. Please. We're fine. Really."

Ralph continued on, but the truth was that they were not fine. Maya had not looked well since they had left the oasis. As Maya leaned her cheek against the pommel, Elissa could see that her eyes were closed. But Elissa knew she was not sleeping. Looking at her little companion, Elissa could plainly see the toll the dry desert heat had taken on Maya over the last few weeks. Her eyes had sunken into dark little pockets, and they had lost their shine. For Maya's sake, she hoped that Ralph had an accurate sense of distance.

"What is it?" asked Maya drowsily.

"We'll be there soon," said Elissa. She patted Maya gently. Maya sighed and closed her eyes again.

Elissa sighed, too. Once they reached Al-hamazar, their journey together would come to an end. She was going to miss Maya more than words could tell. Maya was her only true friend—besides Gertrude, that is. Why, if it hadn't been for Maya, thought Elissa, the buzzards would be playing tiddlywinks with her teeth right now. Or they would both have been captured by that shark-toothed spy, Kreel, and sent back to the Khan. Elissa thought of the Khan: his sadism, his dreadful leer, those fat fingers shoving the remains of some poor, unfortunate creature between his drooping, greasy lips—not to mention what he'd had in store for Maya. Elissa shivered in spite of the heat. Dear little Maya. They'd been through so much together.

"What will you do when you get home?" asked Elissa wistfully. "I bet everyone will throw a big party for you."

Maya opened her eyes. "Oh, I don't know," she said. "I've been gone for such a long time."

"It can't have been that long," said Elissa. "You're not that old."

Maya gave Elissa one of her veiled little smiles. "I've been gone longer than you think," she said. "But they won't have forgotten me." She lapsed into silence.

As always, Maya was vague about her family. Elissa assumed that she simply didn't remember much about her homeland. After all, she had been sold to the Khan when she was just a small child. Still, the little girl was an enigma to Elissa. There were many things she did not understand: her ability to speak half a dozen languages, her self-sufficiency—and, of course, there was Maya's inexplicable talent for locating water, no matter what the distance. Elissa knew that most animals could smell water, but she had never encountered that ability in a person.

But in spite of the mysteries surrounding her, Maya was the one person who accepted Elissa for who she was—Gift and all. She didn't seem to think that Elissa's chatting with a camel was any more unusual than her talking to a person. Of course it wasn't. If anything, animals were easier to converse with. When you talked to an animal, you knew exactly where you stood. They told the truth. Unlike people. Unlike her father . . .

"You're awfully quiet," said Maya.

Elissa looked up, startled. Maya was regarding her with dark eyes.

"Oh," said Elissa. "It's just that I am going to miss you."

"I'm going to miss you, too," said Maya. She twisted around to give Elissa a one-armed hug.

"Something else is bothering you. Your face is all scrunched up."

"It's my father," Elissa confessed.

"Are you having doubts?" asked Maya.

Maya's perceptions frequently amazed Elissa. She could only nod.

"Well," said Maya. "You won't know until you find him."

"That's true," Elissa conceded. She had realized a while ago that her doubts would not be laid to rest until she heard the truth from Falk's own lips. The problem was that the truth, at least in Falk's case, could be awfully complicated. All she really wanted was a straightforward and simple "I love you." Instead she was bound to get long explanations, defenses, lessons in politics—and she didn't really want to explain any of that to Maya. Nor did she want to explain how complex her own feelings had become.

"Finding him isn't going to be easy," Elissa said finally. "I don't know where he is. He said he was fighting a war with his cousin, but he didn't say exactly where."

"That could be a problem," said Maya. She

chewed thoughtfully on the end of her braid. "Wars are bad."

Elissa didn't need to be told how bad wars were. Her own experience with armed conflict had been limited—just a brief skirmish, really. But that had been frightening enough.

"Oh dear," she said. "What shall I do?" Elissa wasn't sure if she should press on or simply wait for the war to end. Anyhow, where would she wait? The world was a big place, and without Maya it was going to get even bigger and much emptier.

"I have an idea," said Maya. "Why don't you come home to the islands with me? You can find your father when his war is over."

"But how will we know when it's over?" asked Elissa. She wondered if there would be some sort of announcement—as for a birth or a coming-of-age.

"My people know everything," said Maya confidently. "They'll help you find him, too."

"Would they do that for me?"

"Of course," said Maya. "Why not?"

Elissa smiled. Maya was so uncomplicated. In

her world, people didn't need to have reasons. Maya just followed her feelings regardless of what other people thought, and she expected everybody else to do the same. Although now that Elissa considered things more carefully, Maya might just have a point. There would be further advantages to delaying her encounter with Falk just a little bit longer. For one thing, Elissa wasn't quite sure how she would be received. Falk might be angry that she hadn't waited for him to return to the Citadel. Once he won his war—and she was sure that he would emerge the victor, Falk being the sort of person who never lost a battle— he might not be as cross with her. And for another thing . . . she just couldn't bear to say goodbye.

"All right, then," she said. "I'll go home with you. To Suleskerry."

Maya didn't answer. Her attention, always somewhat limited, had already drifted on to something else. "What's that?" she asked. Maya was pointing ahead of them at a strangely shaped dune. "It looks like a wall."

It did indeed. As they drew closer, they began

to spot the edges of cracked roof tiles and other debris emerging from the sand.

"I wonder why anyone would want to live out here," mused Elissa. "There's no water at all."

"There was," said Maya with certainty. "This didn't used to be a desert. Ask Ralph about it," she urged.

Elissa loved the fact that she could talk to Ralph and Gertrude openly while they traveled. This was one of the advantages to traveling single file—no one else could overhear them. It was a very good thing they were out of earshot, too, for Maya insisted on having Elissa "translate" everything Ralph and Gertrude said. Elissa was beginning to understand some of the pitfalls of being a translator. Ralph's jokes, for one thing, were just awful.

"Why are you smiling?" asked Maya. "Is he saying something funny about me?" Maya glared at Ralph suspiciously.

"No, no." Elissa hugged Maya exuberantly. "I am just glad to be *your* translator—for once."

Maya smiled up at Elissa. "So, what did he say?"

"I haven't asked him yet." She patted Ralph on his hump to get his attention. Ralph tore himself away from Gertrude, who wasn't in a mood to chat anyway.

"Maya says this wasn't always a desert," Elissa said.

Ralph adopted a scholarly tone. "What the young lady says is true," he said. "At one time this was farmland. Over the last few years, drought and storms have eroded the farmland and allowed the desert to advance at a rapid rate. I myself have seen it." He swung his long face around to look at Maya. "The young lady is very clever. Is she, by any chance, part camel?"

Elissa laughed.

"What did he say?" demanded Maya.

"He said that before the drought this used to be farmland."

"What's so funny about that?" Maya frowned, trying to make the connection.

"He wanted to know if you were part camel."

Maya snorted almost as expressively as Gertrude.

"Just as I thought," said Ralph. He resumed

his rolling gait, and within a few moments the remains of the farm were no longer distinguishable from the sea of sand that had consumed it.

Something about what Ralph had said struck a chord in Elissa. She remembered her father's story about droughts in Castlemar. He had told her they had all but destroyed the silk industry. There had been early frosts in High Crossing for the past several years, too. Early frosts in the valley were always the result of scant rainfall. Ralph's explanation for the spread of the desert seemed to fit in, somehow.

Elissa's thoughts were interrupted by the sound of someone shouting. Far ahead of them, the lead camel had stopped. All the other camels were plodding to the top of a rise. When they reached the crest, the caravan came to a halt. The caravan leader, Jamil, was waving at Ralph and the girls to catch up. Jamil, a tall, reserved man who rarely expressed any sort of emotion, was shouting and swinging his arms over his head in broad arcs.

"What's going on?" asked Elissa.

"Patience, my dear lady," replied Ralph. "Soon you will see."

Ralph lurched onward and upward to the top of the next dune, from which they could see the rest of the caravan etched against the sky in a straggling silhouette. Beyond them rose a magnificent range of mountains. The sight of those jagged, snowcapped peaks was breathtaking, but most wondrous of all were the dozens of slender spires rising white and shimmering in the distance. Fantastically, for they could not be nearly as tall as the mountains behind them, each spire seemed to be encircled by its own cloud. After having seen nothing but dunes and sky in recent weeks, Elissa thought she must be witnessing a mirage. But the spires did not waver or shift in the strong desert light. Ralph stopped for a moment to allow his passengers to admire the view.

"Welcome to Alhamazar," said the camel.

⊸ 2 ⊸

Serena

"I hadn't expected such a big city," said Elissa. Somehow she had always pictured Alhamazar as a larger version of the market at High Crossing—much larger, of course. But this grand, elegant city was beyond all her expectations.

"Indeed," replied Ralph. "Alhamazar is famed for its numerous temples. The first Sultan of Alhamazar built them for his only daughter. She was his pride and joy, the apple of his eye, the cream of his crop. It is said that once, when she requested a cold drink, he sent porters all the way up the sides of the mountains just to bring back chunks of ice for her. Charming tale, don't you think?"

The mountains looked far too imposing to make a trip up and back in a single day, but Elissa wouldn't mind it if someone made the attempt for her. She could use some ice.

"Water!" cried Maya. She had roused herself and was excitedly pointing toward a wide river.

"Does the river run close to Alhamazar?" asked Elissa. She was hoping for Maya's sake that it did.

"Yes, indeed," said Ralph. "The Serena flows alongside its outer boundaries. As we approach the city, you may see the docks."

Elissa followed the course of the river, attempting to pick out jetties, boats, human traffic, but the river soon disappeared in a tangle of vegetation.

"Where does it go?" she asked.

"Why, to the Great Sea, of course," said Ralph. "To Gravesport."

Elissa sucked in her breath. In spite of the fact that she had no idea how she was going to get there, the prospect of seeing the ocean was exciting.

"What is it?" asked Maya.

Elissa gestured toward the river. "That's our way home," she said simply, though this fact hardly needed pointing out. Unless they crossed back through the desert and over the mountains, there was no other way to reach Maya's islands, or, for that matter, Castlemar—whenever that lonesome journey might take place.

As the spires of Alhamazar drew closer, Elissa hoped they would pass through the peaked gates of the inner walls directly into the heart of Old Alhamazar. Instead, the caravan skirted to the north, where the Blue People prepared to make camp for the night. By now the pack animals had clumped together, which made it impossible for Elissa to ask Ralph where they were going or what they were doing. But in this case, she hardly needed his assistance. Her nose told her everything she needed to know.

"Grass!" she cried joyfully. Before her stretched several large open fields. Elissa had spent so many weeks breathing the light, thin desert air that she had almost forgotten the rich, complex odors of vegetation. *But nobody ever really forgets the smell of earth,* she thought, inhaling deeply. The cool, musty odor of well-watered soil, of cropped grass and tangy clover; the sweet scent of flowers; the *greenness* of it all nearly overpowered Elissa. She sneezed violently. Maya was squirming in her seat, anxious to be off the camel. She had smelled water and now must find it.

As Ralph made his way through the field, they passed a group of gaily striped tents sporting flags and banners in all sorts of bright colors—purple and magenta; green and orange; red and blue; silver, copper, and gold. After the monotonous dull yellow of the dunes, the many-hued tents were a feast for the eyes. A dark-haired child wearing an old-fashioned white dress smiled and waved to them from an open cart as they passed by. Elissa smiled back. Once they reached the far corner of the field, the Blue People unloaded the camels and started the process of pitching their sand-colored tents. Maya hopped off Ralph even before he had completely settled to the ground. By the time Elissa had descended, Maya had disappeared.

"Where's she gotten to now?" Elissa muttered. Elissa cast her eyes around for Gertrude, finally locating her in a little pasture next to the water trough. She was rolling in the clover. Flinging off her boots, Elissa ran through the damp cropped grass.

"Want to go exploring with me?" whispered Elissa.

"Sorry, Ralph and I have a dinner date," replied Gertrude, nodding toward a knot of camels who were filling up at the trough. "I'm just getting tidied up." She held a daisy between her teeth.

"Here," offered Elissa. "Let me do that for you." She placed the flower behind Gertrude's ear and gave her a pat on the rump.

"Don't wait up for me," said Gertrude amiably as she ambled off toward the trough.

Elissa stood there for a moment or two, brushing her feet over the fragrant clover that Gertrude had crushed. *Green, how I love you,* she thought. Then, impulsively, she knelt down and kissed the earth.

"What are you doing?"

Elissa looked up into the dark, inquisitive eyes of a small girl. The child was regarding her with a serious, though not unfriendly, expression. She was an adorable child, plump-cheeked and clearly well cared for, for she had just received a thorough scrubbing. Her shiny black hair was still wet from her recent wash. Noting the elaborate cut of the white dress the child was wearing, Elissa realized that this was the little girl who had waved to them from the cart.

"Oh," said Elissa. "I am just showing my appreciation."

"Are you an Erdite?" asked the girl.

Elissa didn't know what an Erdite was, so she answered cautiously. Erdites might be dangerous. "I'm not from here," she explained. "What do Erdites do?"

"They kiss the earth," said the girl unhelpfully. Elissa hoped that, at the very least, the practice of kissing the earth was not considered a sign of insanity.

"They also go to the Erdite temple and light incense to the Earth deities," continued the girl, correctly assessing that Elissa was not a member of that particular sect. "You can't go into their temple unless you bring a gift. I'm not an Erdite, either," she added.

"What are you, then?" Elissa was curious. Religion had not held an especially important place in the affairs of High Crossing. There were little altars and shrines all over, of course—near the river, in the mountains, in kitchens, and in graveyards. But aside from births, deaths, and coming-of-age ceremonies, invoking the gods was a strictly private matter. In other parts of the world, things were no doubt different. Elissa had no wish to offend anyone with her ignorance and hoped that the directness of her question would not be taken as an insult.

"I'm everything!" said the little girl. She threw her hands up in a charming shrug, as if to say, *I just can't help it!*

Elissa breathed a sigh of relief. At least they had something in common. Elissa couldn't help what she was, either. Perhaps she had made a new friend. The little girl, with her round eyes and dimpled cheeks, was precious. She was bright as a button, too. Maybe she could tell Elissa something about the city.

"Are there many temples in Alhamazar?" Elissa prompted, hoping the little girl would tell her more.

The girl looked at Elissa with pretty disdain, as if she had just discovered a particularly stupid variety of lichen. Then she turned and waved her hand toward the city. The spires, touched by the late afternoon sun, were now tinted a shade of pale pink. They were breathtakingly beautiful. Just at that moment, Elissa heard a soft clang, as from a muffled bell, and clouds appeared. No, they weren't clouds. They were flocks of birds—thousands and thousands of white doves, circling the tips of the spires. Elissa clapped her hands together, delighted. Clouds of birds!

"Evening devotions," said the girl.

Elissa turned her head to follow the birds as they made their expansive looping sweeps against the sky.

Elissa turned back to the girl, who was standing very still, looking toward a stand of weeping willows. For the first time, Elissa noticed that water was dripping from the hem of the girl's skirts. She had probably dressed and run off before her mother had had a chance to dry her properly. It was a good thing the air was so warm, or the little thing might catch a chill.

"What's your name?" asked Elissa.

The little girl looked down at the ground, suddenly shy. "My real name?" she asked.

Elissa thought for a moment. Perhaps it was not polite to ask. "Whatever name you would like to tell me," she replied.

The girl leaned close and whispered, "Serena."

"Oh," said Elissa. "Like the river."

The girl nodded gravely. "It was named after me," she said. "Now the river will always be your friend."

Elissa smiled. Children were so sweetly self-important.

"I am Elissa," she said. As if in confirmation, she heard her own name being called even as she said it: *"Eliiiiisssaaa!"* She turned toward the sound, which seemed to be coming from the stand of willows. Maya was just emerging from their midst.

"I have to go now," said the child, starting to walk away. "Come visit." She pointed at one of the closer striped tents. At its peak fluttered a red flag.

"Please, don't go yet," begged Elissa. "That's just my friend." Maya would love to play with this sweet little child. Elissa turned to wave toward Maya. "Over here!" she called. "You will like Maya very much," she said, turning back to the little girl. To her surprise, the child had already gone. *She must be a fast runner,* thought Elissa, casting her eyes around the meadow.

Elissa made her way to the stand of trees where Maya was waving. There was no need to ask where she had been; Maya was soaking wet. When Elissa drew near, Maya grabbed her by the hand, an ecstatic smile dancing over her face. Her eyes were bright and shiny, her hair sleek, her cheeks plump and rosy. *Ah,* thought Elissa with relief. *She's back!*

"Come with me," Maya said, leading Elissa through the trees.

Pushing the drooping branches aside, Elissa saw that they were on the banks of the river Serena itself. At this point in its meanderings the river was not yet wide, though, for such a narrow waterway, it was strangely still. Suddenly Elissa wanted nothing more than to plunge into the cool, clear water. She lifted her hands, preparing to throw off her robe, but Maya stopped her.

"Not here," she said. "It's very deep at this spot. And there is a dangerous undercurrent right at the bend. Let's go upstream a little way."

Elissa trusted Maya's judgment about waterways. She'd never in her life seen a better swimmer. She followed Maya along a narrow path, until they came to a sandy little beach. There she cast aside her dusty blue robe and, once down to her shift, dove in. The water was so cold it made her gasp, but after a few breathless moments she adjusted to the temperature.

"Mountain water," said Maya, who, naturally, had slithered in behind Elissa. Maya could never get enough of the water. Given half a chance, Elissa believed Maya would prefer to eat and sleep in it, too. But unlike Maya, Elissa couldn't stay in the water forever. After a few minutes, she clambered onto the shore and found a smooth, flat rock to stretch out on. Even though the light was waning, the rock had accumulated enough heat during the day to dry the back of her shift within a few moments. Elissa flipped over to dry the front. Pressing her cheek against the warm stone, she closed her eyes in contentment.

Something tickled her face.

Lazily, Elissa propped her chin in her hands. The end of a vine, loosely coiled around the overhanging branches of a tree, had drifted down toward the water. It bore many purple-tipped buds, one of which was now gently poking Elissa's cheek. Elissa sat up, admiring the length of the tightly furled petals. Smiling, she extended her hand to push the vine back, touching the bud lightly with her fingertips.

This bud is going to be one huge flower, she thought. *I wonder what it will look like.*

As she completed her thought, the bud unfurled—slowly, luxuriantly—to become an enormous five-petaled flower. Just as the bud had promised, the flower was a deep purple, its velvety interior speckled with tiny red dots, like delicate freckles. Elissa leaned forward to catch its sweet fragrance. "Ah," she breathed, delighted.

"How did you do that?" Maya had climbed up out of the water to sit on a nearby rock that jutted out from the bank like a little step.

Elissa shrugged. "I didn't do anything," she said. "I was just thinking how pretty the flower would look. Then I reached out." Elissa looked down at her hands, fanning out her fingers as if they were entirely unfamiliar to her.

Maya tilted her head. "How about that one?" she asked.

"This one?" asked Elissa, pointing at the bud next to the opened flower. "It will probably look just like the other—"

Before Elissa could finish her sentence, the bud opened. The flower seemed to droop a little lower. Elissa drew her hand back and the flower raised itself again.

"There must be a little animal climbing up the vine," she said, peering up into the branches of the tree.

"Uh-uh," said Maya, shaking her head. "Do it again."

Elissa reached toward a third bud, again imagining its beauty, and it dipped toward her hand and opened.

"You see?" Maya jumped up excitedly. "You're doing that!"

Elissa lowered her hand. "Sohar didn't say anything about the waters giving people permanent . . ." Elissa faltered, not knowing what word to use. *Powers?*

"Maybe it's not the waters," said Maya. "It could just be you. After all, the animals obey you."

"That's different," said Elissa, although at this point she wasn't entirely sure that it was. "They are my friends."

"Well, they listen to you, and they certainly don't listen to me!" said Maya. She twirled the tip of her braid around her finger, thinking. "Maybe now the plants are your friends, too. Maybe they *have* to obey you."

"But I wasn't even *asking* for anything," Elissa protested. "It's not the way it was at the oasis." Elissa closed her eyes, trying to remember exactly what she had done. The soldiers were all standing before her, holding their weapons, poised to strike. She had told the trees that there was water. "Come and drink," she had said. She had *spoken,* hadn't she? "I *told* the trees what to do then. This time I was just thinking."

"Well, maybe they can read your thoughts now."

Elissa was silent for a moment. "That may not be a good thing."

"Why not?" asked Maya. "If you can make flowers bloom, you can probably make them bud, too. Maybe you can make seeds sprout. That would be good for farmers."

"Not really," said Elissa slowly. "Every plant has its own cycle. It's not a good idea to force things. What if I made the seeds sprout when it was still too cold? The little seedlings would all die."

"I suppose so," said Maya thoughtfully. "You'll have to be careful what you wish for."

Elissa nodded. "Nana used to say that." She dropped her voice, widening her eyes theatrically. "Watch out, you're becoming an old woman." Elissa passed her hands in front of Maya.

Maya bent over, pretending to lean on a cane and screwing up her eyes comically, which made Elissa giggle. Still laughing, the girls threw on their robes and raced back to the camp.

By now the tents were all pitched and smoke was rising up in lazy drifts from the cooking fires. There was a look of contentment on the faces of the Blue People. They had reached their destination safely, and all was well. The men sat back on their haunches and told jokes while they waited for their suppers.

The two girls ate dinner in their tent—succulent fried bean patties and bowls of rice—then stretched out to rest.

"Maya," said Elissa, "do you remember that little child who waved at us when we first came?"

"No," said Maya, yawning. "I don't."

"Maybe you were looking in the other direction." *Maya was probably looking toward the river,* Elissa thought. After weeks in the desert, nobody could blame her. Elissa continued, "Well, the girl you didn't see invited us to come to her tent tonight."

"Which tent?" asked Maya, now interested.

"One of the striped tents," said Elissa.

"Oh," said Maya, nodding. "She's probably a Mender child, then."

"A what?" asked Elissa.

"Menders," repeated Maya patiently. "They go from place to place. Haven't you seen them before?" She didn't wait for Elissa to reply. "They travel around, fixing things—pots and pans, broken wheels, anything that's hard to mend. They have a knack for it. And they read fortunes, too. Don't they come up North?"

"Yes, I believe they do," replied Elissa. "But they sleep in covered wagons, not tents. They usually keep to themselves, although young people like to visit them to buy love charms. We call them Tinkers, but I suppose they're probably the same people, because they fix things."

"Yes, those are Menders," confirmed Maya. She looked out the tent flap. "It's getting dark, so if you want to go see that girl, we'd better leave soon."

"Do you think we should tell Jamil where we are going?" asked Elissa.

"No, it's late. If we ask, he probably won't let us go," said Maya. "He's afraid we'll be stolen again."

That was precisely the thought on Elissa's mind. But with the Khan defeated, what was there to be afraid of? She stood up. "Well then, let's go!"

The two girls slipped out through the tent flap and hurried away from camp unnoticed. By now it was twilight. The sleepy evening chatter of birds drifted up from the riverbank. It was a sound Elissa had not heard in a long, long time. "Good night!" the birds called softly to one another. "All's well." Elissa yawned. It would be good to be pressed up against the soft, springy turf tonight, with the rustling of leaves lulling her to sleep.

Fortunately, the Mender camp wasn't too far

away. The Menders had arranged their carts and tents to form a rough circle, within which numerous small fires flickered softly. Men and women sat together, talking quietly or playing games, while children ran around in small packs, playing Find Me. The sweet sound of a guitar floated between the tents, seeming to come from everywhere and nowhere all at once.

"Which tent did she say?" asked Maya.

A small boy careened into Elissa's skirts.

"Do you know where I can find the tent with the red flag?" she asked. The boy laughed and ran off. Perhaps the Menders did not speak Common Tongue.

"That way," said a voice from behind them.

Elissa turned to see a dark-eyed young man leaning against one of the carts. He had a guitar in one hand. With the other, he pointed to their left.

"Thank you," said Elissa. The young man smiled but did not reply.

As they walked in the direction the young man had indicated, Elissa peered up at the peaks of the tents. In the failing light, she couldn't quite make out the colors of the flags—red was already turning to black. Then she saw a portly woman emerge from one of the tents. She was wearing a white lace-trimmed blouse and striped skirts that billowed straight out from her wide waist, so that they seemed to form a tent of their own. A white scarf was wrapped around her head. To Elissa she looked reassuringly matronly and very clean. This might be Serena's mother.

"Pardon me," began Elissa. "I am looking for a little girl—" She hesitated. The way Serena had said, "My real name?" might mean that true names should not be revealed. "Dark-haired," she said, extending her palm level with her hip to indicate a very small child.

"White dress?" asked the woman.

"Yes," said Elissa happily. "Is this the right place?"

"Could be," said the woman vaguely, but she flashed them a welcoming smile. In the darkness, her smile seemed to cast a light of its own. The woman held the tent flap aside for them to pass through.

The interior of the tent was surprisingly

spacious. Or perhaps that was an illusion, for so many veils hung from the ceiling that Elissa's view of the interior of the tent was obscured. From what Elissa could see of it, the place was comfortably furnished. In a far corner, a bed was covered with a handsome rug. A large carved chest was pushed against the footboard. At the center of the tent stood a low table, around which were clustered several stools. Placing a lit candle on the table, the woman beckoned the girls to sit.

"Now, what bring you to Mama?" she asked. The candlelight flickered off her brilliant smile.

Elissa was confused. "Where is your daughter?" she asked. "She told us to come visit."

For some reason, the woman found Elissa's question hilarious. She gave a big belly laugh that shook her chins and made the veils hanging from the ceiling flutter. "I have no daughter," she said finally. "Just me live here."

Elissa started to rise. "Oh, I am sorry. I was looking for the tent with the red flag."

The woman waved her hand for Elissa to sit again. "This right place. I be Mama Red Flag. Nobody else go by that name." Mama Red

Flag's face was still creased in a smile, but her eyes were serious. "Now, why she send you to Mama, I wonder." As the woman did not seem to be asking this question of Elissa or of Maya, the two girls remained silent. The woman clasped her hands together over her ample bosom.

"Thank you!" she cried suddenly, lifting her hands up toward the ceiling. "You send Mama good Sign!" Then she looked at Elissa. "Show Mama left hand," she ordered.

Elissa felt a little awkward giving her hand to this stranger, but the woman looked so pleasant and friendly, surely no harm would come of it. Instead of looking at her hand, the woman simply held it, with her eyes shut. Giving her head a little shake, as if rousing herself from a dream, she turned it palm up and peered at it intently. Then she turned it over and examined the back. Finally, closing it into a loose fist, she stared at the sides. When she was done, she turned it palm up again, sighing contentedly.

"I give you good Destiny," she announced at last. "You meet tall, dark, handsome stranger and be mama to many children. You stay on right path. You go very far. It be good for whole world." Elissa smiled; the woman probably said the same thing to everybody.

Then Mama Red Flag asked for Maya's hand. Like Elissa, Maya hesitated.

"Go ahead," Elissa encouraged her. "It doesn't hurt."

Reluctantly, Maya extended her hand. The woman took it gently, as she had Elissa's, but when she looked at it, she sucked in her breath. She turned Maya's hand over—once, twice. Then, with shining eyes, she gave it back.

"Ah!" she exclaimed, her eyes wide. "I see you now, little Silky! What you be doin' in that skin? You not be hidin' from Mama Red Flag!" she admonished. Then she leaned forward. "Will you give Mama Red Flag blessing of the Waters?" she asked humbly.

Maya glanced at Elissa, who shrugged but nevertheless smiled reassuringly and whispered, "Go ahead." Mama Red Flag was a little odd, but Elissa was sure she meant no harm.

Maya stood up. Then she leaned over and,

placing her small hands on the woman's head, kissed her formally in the center of her forehead. Mama Red Flag beamed ecstatically.

"Aren't you going to tell her fortune?" asked Elissa.

Mama Red Flag leaned back, still smiling broadly, and crossed her arms over her stomach. "Can only read human hand," she said.

Elissa frowned, not understanding. Maya was nothing if not a little girl, and, in most respects, a completely typical one at that—talkative, fidgety, and easily distracted. Elissa dismissed Mama Red Flag's refusal to read Maya's palm as an eccentricity. She suspected that fortune-tellers were not best known for their logic. Instead of reason, they probably relied upon intuition, clairvoyance, second sight—all those things that cannot be explained.

The girls made their thanks and got up to go. As they were about to leave, a thought occurred to Elissa. "Where is the child?" she asked. "The one who sent us here."

"Serena?" inquired the woman.

Elissa nodded, somehow not surprised that Mama Red Flag would know the girl's true name.

"Ah," said Mama Red Flag, lifting her fore-finger. "You not be seeing her again."

Elissa wondered how Mama Red Flag would know that. "Why not?" she asked.

Mama Red Flag rose and ushered the girls to the entrance to the tent as she spoke: "That child be Serena Alhamazar, only daughter of First Sultan. She drown in that river two hundred year ago. Her daddy grieve so much for his sweet baby, he build a temple to each god. And he name that river after her."

As the girls passed into the night, the tent flap fell softly behind them, like a sigh.

↬ 3 ↫

The Finest Length of Silk

Elissa slept so deeply that night that when the following day dawned with the direct, no-nonsense light of the South, she was almost sure the events of the previous evening had been a dream. After poking her head out of the tent flap, her belief was confirmed. There wasn't a single striped tent in view. Perhaps she was suffering from some of the residual effects of sunstroke. In a way, it was reassuring to think she'd had a hallucination. Given the amount of time they'd spent in the desert, sunstroke was an entirely plausible explanation, and she much preferred it over thinking that yesterday she'd had a conversation with a ghost and that her dearest friend, Maya, wasn't human.

"The Menders must have left before dawn,"

said Maya, destroying Elissa's attempt at self-delusion. She sniffed the breeze. "Breakfast is ready."

Elissa and Maya wandered over to the breakfast fires and gobbled up their date-sweetened gruel in companionable silence, food and daylight reducing the events of the previous night to a strange, but essentially harmless, experience. Fortune-tellers and ghost stories—these were merely entertainments for an evening, not cause for alarm. In any event, today everything but Alhamazar had been erased from their minds. They were both very much looking forward to a trip to the market that morning. Especially Elissa. Today was an important day, and not just because they had finally reached Alhamazar.

"What do you want for your birthday?" Maya asked innocently.

"I thought you forgot!" Elissa had mentioned her birthday several days ago, but Maya had a notoriously loose sense of time.

"I counted!" said Maya, proudly holding up her hands and wiggling her fingers. Then she swept an imaginary hat from her head and bowed deeply from the waist, proclaiming, "Today, mistress, I will give you anything you desire." Maya tilted her head to the side and winked at Elissa. "How about a tall, dark, handsome stranger? I'm sure I can find you one in the market."

Elissa laughed. "You couldn't afford one. You have no money." She paused, thinking of Nana's gold coins, as yet unspent. "But I do."

"Good!" said Maya enthusiastically. "You can pick out your present and pay for it. And then I will give it to you!"

Elissa smiled at the absurdity of being handed such a "gift," but Maya was right. The occasion demanded a purchase.

"I'll get something for both of us." Elissa felt just as much excitement at the idea of wandering through Alhamazar's legendary market as Maya did. "We'll walk to the market a little later."

"Perhaps not," whispered Maya, glancing past Elissa. "Look who's coming."

Jamil, the caravan leader, was making his way across the encampment. As he approached, the girls rose to greet him. Jamil inclined his head and dropped his eyes respectfully. He spoke first, his face, as always, grave. Elissa, whose command of Tamayat merely extended to basic greetings, only understood "Good morning."

"He says we need to get ready to leave." Maya translated Jamil's words softly, disappointment evident in her voice.

"Why so soon?" asked Elissa.

"There is a cargo boat leaving for Gravesport early this afternoon. He wants to secure us passage this morning, before they finish loading up."

Elissa understood the concern of the caravan leader. Once they were safely aboard a vessel, his duty would be completed. Yet opportunities like Alhamazar did not come every day. In fact, for people from High Crossing, they came once in a lifetime—if at all. Elissa was about to propose a brief shopping expedition on their way to the boat, but the look in the Blue man's eye stopped her. Given Elissa's importance, not to mention the previous difficulty the Blue People had experienced transporting these girls to their destination, he obviously wished to take no risks. And Jamil, with his sharp face and sharper knife, was not someone Elissa wished to cross.

The girls gathered up their belongings and

followed the leader to the edge of the clearing, where Gertrude awaited them. She had been fed and watered, yet judging from the droop of her ears and the downcast expression of her eyes, she was not happy.

"Ralph says 'adieu,'" Gertrude muttered, disconsolate. Elissa gave her a sympathetic pat.

They walked in silence through the outskirts of the city, which were pressed right up against the city walls. The dwellings they passed were for the most part plain white houses surrounding open, dirt-floored courtyards. At the center of each courtyard stood a large square basin surrounded by tubs. Elissa guessed that these courtyards were habitually used as washing areas. She was proven right when she saw a small child emerge, dripping, from one of the tubs. The houses looked surprisingly humble, given Alhamazar's fame. As they walked by, flocks of young children, virtually naked, rushed toward them, hands outstretched. Jamil swatted them away, clearly annoyed. The Blue People did not approve of begging.

As they continued along the well-worn path, the compounds disappeared, to be replaced by more substantial-looking buildings. These, Elissa guessed, were probably used as safeholds or warehouses, as the doors bore formidable locks and bars. The windows, each of which faced the front, were all barred as well. Elissa wondered what was inside the buildings, but there was no time to ask. Jamil was striding along at such a pace that it was hard to keep up with him. Stopping was clearly out of the question.

Eventually the path wound its way past the storehouses to the docks that formed the eastern boundary of Alhamazar. Elissa looked toward the city walls, above which she could make out the tops of some of the taller spires. Even from this distance, she could see that they were beautifully carved. As she watched, a flock of white doves emerged and flew in a lazy circle around the tip of the tallest spire before settling back into the tower's nooks and crannies. Elissa watched them in frustration. She was so close and yet so far.

Jamil, looking straight ahead, advanced with purpose toward the docks. Several vessels were being loaded with goods and livestock, but the one that caught Elissa's eye was a brightly striped red and blue barge. Apparently this was to be their transport, for it was here that Jamil stopped. He called out an inquiry to the men on deck. Within a few moments, the Captain himself came down to meet them. After exchanging a few words in Tamayat with the caravan leader, he nodded his assent.

"We'll take good care of them," he said in Common Tongue, leaning over to pat Elissa and Maya on their heads. Elissa noticed that he glanced at the fibula she was wearing as he spoke, so she was sure that the Captain would be true to his word. He probably had had enough dealings with Blue People in the past to know that thwarting their desires would not bode well.

Jamil said a few formal words before he departed and then, facing the girls, bowed low. Without waiting for them to speak, he touched his forehead and strode away.

The Captain cleared his throat. "You don't see that every day," he said, nodding toward Jamil's retreating back. "You must have done something impressive to deserve a bow like that. Not to mention the blessing of Ankaa." He squinted down at the girls. Elissa and Maya exchanged a brief look.

When the girls didn't answer, the Captain introduced himself. "I'm Jarvison," he said.

"I'm Elissa, and this is Maya." As Elissa spoke, she watched Jamil disappear between the storehouses, his robe flapping sharply against his tall, spare frame. Unexpectedly, she felt a small pang. The Blue People were hard to know at first, but they were loyal and true and could be counted on in difficult situations.

"Don't worry," said the Captain. "You'll be safe with me."

Elissa believed that. Captain Jarvison was a powerful-looking man with a full black beard. Elissa suspected that he never had any discipline problems with his crew. His hands looked strong enough to rip a man in two. He crooked a finger the size of a ninepin at a sailor who was coiling a lanyard. The sailor instantly dropped his rope and led them to a cabin, while another led the unprotesting Gertrude to the hold. The cabin was neat but tiny, with barely enough room for two narrow bunks and a small closet. Once their belongings were securely stowed away, the young sailor turned and closed the door firmly behind him.

The girls sat on their bunks, looking at the bare walls. There was no porthole. After spending so many weeks in the vast, open expanse of the desert, Elissa felt acutely confined. "I wonder exactly when we'll be leaving," she said.

"I heard one of the sailors say we'd be loaded up by early afternoon," replied Maya. "I think we are the only passengers." She yawned. "I am going to take a nap."

Within a few minutes, Maya's soft breathing filled the cabin. It had been a long week. And a longer winter. Elissa took off her blue desert robe and stretched out, trying to fall asleep herself. But try as she might, sleep would not come. Here she was, a stone's throw from the Alhamazar market. How could she sleep? And it was her birthday! Lying in the bottom of a dingy old boat was no way to celebrate her fourteenth year. Elissa sat up. Noon was still a couple of hours away. If she hurried, she could make it back before anyone noticed her absence. She slipped quietly from her bunk and put on her robe and boots. There was no point in waking Maya; the poor thing was exhausted. Besides, Elissa would be back in no time—with a gift for both of them. What had Mama Red Flag called Maya? "Silky"? Elissa smiled in anticipation of Maya's delight when she returned with a full length of silk.

Carefully, Elissa sat back down and opened her pack, removing her homespun cloak. Holding up the hem, she broke a few of the threads with her teeth until she could see the edge of a gold coin. She eased it out carefully. Elissa held the heavy coin in her hand for a moment, weighing it. Now, where to hide it? Pockets could be picked. Elissa slipped the coin into her boot, where it lodged itself firmly next to her instep. Then she tugged the loose threads to draw the hem tight again and shoved the cloak back into her pack.

She rose to her feet silently, unhooking the fibula from the shoulder of her blue desert robes. Although the fibula had its purposes, for this task it wouldn't do for her to stand out too much. For that matter, it would probably be better to remove the blue robes, too, as she was not a Blue person. The robes had served their purpose in the desert, but in the market she would probably be better off wearing something more ordinary. She rummaged through her pack, encountering first the pink silk gown Maya had made for her—pretty but not practical—and then her blouse and skirt. These would do, as would the black hooded robe she'd brought from the Citadel.

After donning her clothes, Elissa pushed her cloak and the blue robes under her blankets, molding them to form an Elissa-shaped mound. There! If any nosy sailors came to check on them, she'd be fast asleep—just like Maya. She adjusted the robe around her shoulders and then, almost as an afterthought, slipped Sohar's fibula into her skirt pocket. You never knew what kind of people you would encounter in Alhamazar. And, after all, the lovely pin was meant to protect her, even if not precisely as a weapon. She pulled the hood over her head, assured that she was now completely unrecognizable.

Elissa tiptoed to the door and carefully opened it. No one was about. She hurried quietly through the passageway. When she reached the deck, she poked her head cautiously through the doorway. The oarsmen were busy loading crates into the hold of the ship, their backs to her. In an instant, Elissa was across the deck and down the gangplank. She almost flew onto the dock. Fortunately, there was enough of a crowd to hide her as she scurried away from the barge and into the city. It took all of her will not to run. But it would not do to be taken for a thief; the last thing she wanted was to be returned to the vessel empty-handed and embarrassed. She wove her way carefully through the streets, keeping her eyes focused ahead of her, following the drift of the foot traffic. She suspected that everyone would be headed for the market.

Her hunch paid off. Within a few minutes she found herself at the edge of the market. It was immense, more like a small city than an open market. Vendors' booths stretched as far as the eye could see, their colorful awnings flapping in the breeze. Throngs of people squeezed into the narrow aisles in a steady stream, the vendors crying out the quality of their goods as customers flocked by. Elissa was relieved to hear Common Tongue being spoken. That meant she'd be able to haggle. Elissa hardly considered herself to be an expert haggler, never having had any money to haggle with. But she had seen other people do it at the summer fair in High Crossing and felt she could manage. All she had to do was pretend she knew what she was doing. That should be easy.

Somebody jostled her, making her nervous. Elissa held her robe tightly around her as she entered the market, doubly glad she'd put the gold piece in her boot. She patted the little pouch that hung around her neck for comfort. Even though the shard that lay within it had not been given to her by Nana, she still regarded it as her lucky talisman. Although, when she thought of it, the little silver vial of water from the Sacred Lake was probably more of a protection from the dangers of the world than a chunk of clay.

Elissa made her way through the open aisles. This part of the market was reserved for fishmongers. Given its proximity to the wharves, that made sense. At almost midday, however, the odor was overwhelming. Soon the fishmongers gave way to fruit stalls. Mounds of exotic fruits and vegetables, most of which she had never seen before, were stacked in front of the stalls in bright pyramids of red, yellow, orange, and purple. Bored-looking traders who slowly passed immense fans over the fruit to keep flies away called out to her. Even though her stomach rumbled, Elissa didn't dare stop. She wondered how she was going to locate the section reserved for silk in time to return to the boat. At this rate she would hardly be able to find what she needed, let alone buy it. Keeping her head down and plowing straight ahead, like a bull, she entered the heart of the market, where made goods were sold.

The crowds were now so thick that Elissa could hardly see where she was going. With every step she took, someone shoved her in one direction or another. Vendors hurried past her, carrying baskets filled with gaily painted clay cups, silver plates, embossed books, birds, beads, beans, buttons. There were whole aisles devoted to harness makers, saddle makers, soap makers, shoemakers. The noise was deafening. Coppersmiths banged at their shiny plates and bowls; furniture makers hammered at tables, chairs, chests; instrument makers blew horns and whistles. And the smells! The air was thick with a redolent combination of animal hide, incense, perfume, human sweat, and manure. And above the din—people arguing, shouting, and cursing in half a dozen languages—Elissa caught snippets of Tamayat and occasional glimpses of blue robes among the multicolored throngs as she was swept along.

Suddenly the crowds thinned. The aisles in this section of the market were completely shaded by high awnings that blocked out most of the sun. Elissa stopped and listened. Here there was no noise, no bustle—just the soft rustling of cloth floating gently in the slight breeze. Silk.

Elissa was thrilled. What luck! She'd found the silk quarter—and just in time. She looked about her. The booths in this section were completely enclosed, unlike the other stalls. Silk was a delicate and prized item. It would not be prudent to leave it hanging in the open to gather dust and debris from the street. Silk merchants could not afford to have their costly products damaged, as one stain could render an entire length of silk worthless. And unlike other goods, the final selling price of silk could be kept private. From the sheer quantity of booths, Elissa imagined that competition among silk dealers must be fierce. She wandered the length of the aisle, contemplating the various swatches of material that hung above each door. These swatches gave all the information a connoisseur of silk would need.

As she passed a nondescript booth, a well-dressed gentleman emerged, carrying a length of shimmering water. At least that is how it appeared to Elissa. The silk he held up to the light flowed through his fingers in a glistening cascade. He furrowed his brow and reentered the shop. Elissa followed him.

"How can you doubt me?" the merchant was crying. "This is my finest length."

"It has a flaw," insisted the customer, a beefy man with a florid face. "It is not worth the price."

"What flaw? There is no flaw!" The shopkeeper was irate. Elissa sidled closer to the bolt of cloth. She could see why the shopkeeper was upset. It was the finest silk Elissa had ever seen. It spilled and billowed over the counter's edge like sea foam. Its color was difficult to determine, for, like an opal, it seemed to reflect a subtle array of delicate hues. There was not a catch or a run in it. The customer was just being difficult, haggling for a lower price. Elissa knew that if he offended the seller too much, the sale would collapse. She squeezed her eyes shut and clutched her little purse for luck.

"Two silvers, take it or leave it," announced the man huffily.

"Two silvers! It is worth ten times that price! Out, out! Get out!" shouted the merchant. Even though he stood a half head shorter than the customer, the silk dealer escorted the beefy man out, holding his collar with a grip like iron. Elissa waited quietly for the merchant to return—as he soon did, muttering under his breath.

"Don't touch that!" he snapped when he observed Elissa standing next to the counter.

Elissa nodded and waited for him to calm down, which he did as soon as she spoke. "How much for a length?"

The merchant immediately focused on the young girl before him.

"I sell only very fine lengths," he announced with a haughty jerk of his chin. "Perfectly dyed and finished."

"I am sure of that," said Elissa evenly. She did not look at the silk tumbling lustrously only a few inches away from her hand. She was longing to stroke it, to feel it flowing cool and light between her fingers. But she knew that if she expressed too much interest, the merchant would increase the price. "Do you have anything in red?"

The merchant sat on his high stool, looking down at Elissa in a disapproving manner. It was obvious from her plain, dusty robe that she could not afford anything in his store.

"Of course." He turned and removed several bolts, all vibrantly colored, from niches in the wall. "Do you know your silk?"

Elissa did. "These are from Castlemar," she said. "The dyes will never fade or run."

The silk merchant nodded appreciatively as he ran his fingers lovingly over the material. Elissa noticed that his hands were entirely without calluses. Silk merchants probably needed to maintain perfectly smooth skin so as not to damage their merchandise.

She examined the bolts of cloth with polite interest and listened to the merchant describe the beauty of the designs, the perfection of their execution. Then she made a disappointed little sound and apologized. "I'm sorry, I just don't see anything that appeals to me." With a polite

"Good day," she turned to leave. Then, as she was about to exit the shop, she made a casual gesture toward the silk on the counter. "How much for that one?"

The merchant narrowed his eyes. "Girl," he said, "I don't know what kind of game you're playing, but I can't waste any more time with you. *That* is the finest length of silk that has ever crossed my counter, and it is far, far too expensive for the likes of you."

"How much?" Elissa folded her arms and looked the silk merchant in the eye.

The merchant gave Elissa a triumphant look. "A gold."

Elissa was staggered. "That's . . . is *that* your lowest price?"

"That's my only price."

Elissa had no idea silk could be so expensive. But it was clear from the quality of the silk, and from the superior smile on the merchant's face, that he wasn't going to reduce the price. However, it was now her turn to surprise him. She reached down into her boot and withdrew the coin, smiling just slightly at the merchant's expression.

The little man stood with his mouth ajar. When Elissa handed him the coin, he weighed it and then clamped it between his teeth. The slight indentations on the surface of the coin indicated that it was indeed pure gold.

"Sold!" he announced. Elissa watched as he expertly refolded and wrapped the silk in a square of plain linen. He threw in a spool of matching silk thread as a bonus for his "special customer."

"We must seal the purchase," he said, drawing a bottle out from under the counter. Seeing Elissa's expression, he snickered. "It's just tea," he said, then reached under the counter again to find a tiny glass. Filling it from the bottle, he offered it to Elissa with a flourish.

Elissa sniffed at the liquid. Unknown teas always made her nervous. It had a familiar odor. Mint . . . and something else.

"Drink!" he ordered. "For the silk!" Elissa didn't want the tea, and she didn't especially like the sly look on the merchant's face, but time was running short. She downed her drink in a single gulp. It was cloyingly sweet, though the aftertaste was slightly bitter. She thanked the man and hurried out of the shop. The transaction must have taken the better part of an hour. She'd have to rush to make it back to the boat before noon. She did not take the time to greet the florid customer, who was just then reentering the shop. As she hurried away, she heard the shopkeeper's gloating "It's sold!" with only half an ear.

Elissa strode down the shaded aisles of the silk section until they gave way to an open square. She looked up at the sky. It was getting late. Crowds of shoppers rushed by. Suddenly Elissa didn't know which way to turn. Each of the four alleys leading from the market looked the same to her. Had she come from the right or from the left? An old man driving a donkey laden with clay pots pushed past her.

"*Arrefeek!* Get out of the way!"

The donkey muttered something about her load being too heavy.

Elissa was reminded that Gertrude was on the boat, too, waiting for her. She was starting to feel a little frantic. Elissa turned left. The wharves should be to the east, but the sun was so high, she couldn't orient herself. The awnings of the stalls on either side flapped lazily in the breeze—*thwuk, thwuk, thwuk.* The sound was soothing, soporific.

Abruptly the narrow street ended and Elissa stood facing a white wall. She didn't remember this wall; she must have missed a turnoff. Elissa turned left again. By her calculations, the wharves must be very close. This wall must be the back of a large warehouse. The alleyway along the wall was very narrow and entirely deserted. Elissa felt very sleepy. It was lunchtime and she hadn't had anything since dawn, except for the tea. Her legs felt so heavy. She thought that if she sat down for just a moment, her strength would return. She leaned against the wall. The package of silk started to slip from her hands. She needed just a moment off her feet . . .

As Elissa slid to the ground, she heard a familiar cry and knew she was close to the water. The raucous calling of the gulls was the last thing she remembered as she slipped into unconsciousness. "Fish!" they cried. "Fish!" *Always hungry,* she thought. Then everything went dark. She did not even feel the rough gravel beneath her cheek or the hands that pulled off her boots.

∽ 4 ∾

Some Kind of Fancy Sailor

Billy Buck stood in an alley, staring at a blank wall. He had no idea where he was, which, sad to say, was not an unusual predicament for him. He had absolutely no sense of direction. At least that was what Cappy kept telling him. "Bucko, me boy," Cappy had said on more than one occasion, "ye'd lose yerself in yer own bed."

If that's the case, Billy thought, *why couldn't I have just stayed aboard the* Maiden? *Let Cappy find his own crew.* After all, that was what captains were for. Deckhands weren't meant to go roaming around in confusing cities doing things they had no experience at. Deckhands were supposed to do things on deck with their hands. Bailing, for instance; Billy had had plenty of experience at that. He looked up and down the alley, wondering which way to go. The wall offered him no advice.

The truth was that Billy always felt distinctly uncomfortable on land. There was something disorienting about the way land just sat there. It never told you where to go. Water, on the other hand, was a cinch to move around in. It went in one direction or the other, and you went with it. What could be easier?

Billy tramped alongside the wall, disgruntled. Complain as he might, he knew perfectly well why old Cappy couldn't come into town. So did everybody else in Alhamazar, which was the problem. Set one foot on the docks and they'd have him in irons faster than he could yell, "Luff my sails!" And then where would they all be? A ship without a captain wasn't a ship at all. Come to think of it, the *Swamp Maiden* wasn't exactly a ship. Properly speaking, she was more like a contraption. But she floated—most of the time—and that was good enough for everybody aboard. Besides, there was no other crew to spare. Doc was needed at the landing, simply because he had brains and Cappy needed him for all sorts of advice. And so Cappy really had no choice but to pass the job on to Billy, albeit reluctantly.

"First get into the boat and go to town." Cappy had pointed to the skiff and then circled his arms in a rowing gesture. "Dock at the far end. Get out of the boat." The Captain made climbing motions.

Billy bobbed his head, memorizing.

"Go right." The Captain held up his right hand for Billy to see and swept it away from him. "Follow the storehouses until you smell fish." He repeated the motion with his left hand. "Then go left. When yer see the big barrels all lined up in a row, stop. That's the shipyard provisions market. Almost anybody yer see there will be a cook. Hire one. Give him one silver and promise him another at Gravesport."

The Captain handed Billy a leather purse clanking with coins, which Billy stuffed deep into the pocket of his breeches. Billy was big enough so that the Captain didn't have to worry about pickpockets or ruffians. Anybody who saw the breadth of his shoulders and the length of his arms would think twice before tackling Billy. "Oh," the Captain added. "Don't forget to tell him we'll be taking the back way."

"What should I buy?" asked Billy. He didn't know much about cooking. Usually, though, between the three of them they came up with something you could choke down.

"Nothing, dolt!" cried the Captain. "That's what we're hiring a cook for! The cook'll know what provisions to buy. Give him the purse. Once ye've stocked up, *come back with the cook.* Got it?"

Billy had nodded. Getting "it" wasn't the problem. It was getting *there* that confounded him, not to mention the getting *back* part. *Back* was where he ran into real problems. This time he was sure he'd followed the instructions well enough. Left, swoosh of the hand. Right, swoosh of the hand. But somehow he had taken the wrong turn and ended up behind the wharves. Now he was stuck in this lonely little alley. Billy rambled aimlessly past long, dingy walls, mumbling to himself about barrels. It never occurred to him to retrace his steps in order to find his way back to the wharf. Going back wouldn't have helped him anyway. The same route taken twice would have looked completely unfamiliar to Billy Buck.

Billy rounded a corner and stumbled over a bundle of rags. *Now, who would leave a perfectly good bunch of rags lying in an alley?* he thought. He bent over. It was a girl! And from the looks of her, she was fast asleep. No, not asleep. Her breathing was ragged and uneven. Billy turned her over. She was lying on top of a parcel of some sort. And she wasn't wearing any shoes. Her robe was disheveled and all twisted about, as though she had been searched. Billy was sure that if he looked, he wouldn't find a purse. She'd been robbed. He wondered why they had taken her shoes.

Billy touched her shoulder. She mumbled something about fish. Perhaps she was a servant girl sent to purchase some fish for dinner. Billy scratched his head. The fishmongers had all closed up shop at noon. He wondered how long she had been lying there.

Billy didn't stand there thinking for too long. The thieves who had robbed the lass might still be close at hand. He bent down and hoisted the girl up over his broad shoulder and, tucking her parcel securely under his arm, strode down the alleyway. She wasn't heavy. After a few yards, Billy spied a small boot, then another. He picked those up as well. Not long afterward he came upon a little velvet pouch. He felt around inside it. There was no money in it, just a piece of broken pottery and a tiny bottle. The thieves had probably taken her money and thrown the purse aside. *Poor little lass,* Billy thought. *She is going to catch the devil from her mistress when she gets home.* Billy stuffed the pouch inside one of the girl's boots and continued on. After two more turns, Billy found himself back on the wharf, exactly where he had started.

"Well, luff my sails!" he cried. "I've made it back!" Billy was astounded and pleased. He wondered if he'd be able to do it twice, because he'd certainly have to. Cappy had sent him into the city to search for a cook, and so far all he'd found was a barefoot girl. After he took the girl home, he'd have to deal with the maze of streets again.

The girl was starting to stir against his shoulder. Billy marched straight on until he came to a bench set against a warehouse wall. There he set her gently down. She slumped lightly against him, her eyes fluttering a bit. It looked as though she was coming to. Billy fanned her with his cap.

"Wake up, wee missy," Billy called in a soft voice. He gazed down at her. Truth to tell, she didn't look much like a servant girl. Her hands were far too smooth.

Elissa struggled to open her eyes. All at once she sat bolt upright. Where was she? What had happened? Elissa looked wildly around her. She was sitting on a bench next to a very large young man dressed in a red and white striped shirt. He appeared to be swatting at her head with a greasy cap. She drew back, alarmed.

"Who are you? What are you doing?" Elissa looked down at her bare feet. "What did you do with my boots?" She clutched at her neck desperately. "Where is my purse?"

"Nay, miss, I'm no robber! I found yer lyin' back there in the alley." Billy twisted his cap in both hands, his freckled face the image of distress. He handed Elissa her parcel, then placed her boots carefully at her feet, withdrawing the small velvet pouch and holding it out to her.

"I'm sorry, but it looks like they've taken all yer money and left yer with naught but yer little purse." His brow was furrowed in concern.

"I am sorry," she said, slipping the little bag around her neck. "I took you for my assailant."

Billy looked flustered. It seemed she had mistaken him for some kind of fancy sailor. He didn't know whether to nod or shake his head, so he simply stared at her like a man who'd lost his wits. He'd never seen eyes like hers.

"What's your name?" she asked.

The youth reddened. "Billy," he stammered. "Billy Buck."

"I am Elissa." The girl held out her hand. Billy shook it. She grimaced slightly.

"Are yer hurt?" asked Billy kindly.

Elissa nodded cautiously. "I bought a length of silk," she said, gesturing at her package. Billy looked impressed. "I drank some tea at the shop. Then I got so sleepy, I had to sit down."

"The merchant spiked yer tea with poppy juice," said Billy sagely. "It's an old trick. The tea befuddles yer. Then they follow after and rob yer. He must have seen yer purse there in the booth."

"No," explained Elissa. "I put my money in my boot."

Billy gave her an approving look. "That's right smart. Excepting he saw yer take it out, didn't he?"

Elissa looked embarrassed. It had never occurred to her that merchants could be so dishonest. "Why didn't he steal the silk, too?" she asked. "He said it was one of a kind."

"That's right," Billy said. "He couldn't sell it again because the authorities would catch him once yer reported it. Silks are all registered with the authorities, being so valuable."

Elissa nodded with difficulty, remembering the florid man who'd entered the silk merchant's store and the merchant's triumphant "It's sold!" She imagined that the news would travel fast, especially if the silk was as rare as the merchant said it was.

"Yer silvers, on the other hand, can't be traced." The sailor looked sad for her. Then he bent over to help Elissa with her boots. She was still slow from the drugged tea and was having trouble with the laces.

"We'll go straightaway to the Market Master and lodge a complaint," he said as he tied her laces into knots that wouldn't come loose in a hurricane. "They'll haul in the old trickster and get yer money back."

"He didn't take anything," said Elissa.

Billy straightened up. "Say? But yer purse was empty! Save a perfume bottle and a little bit o' clay . . ." He flushed slightly at the admission that he'd searched her belongings. But Elissa didn't look at all perturbed by what he'd said.

"I wasn't carrying any money," she explained. "I left the rest in—" Panicked, Elissa leapt to her feet. "My ship!" she cried. She grabbed her package and started to run toward the wharves. Billy trotted after her.

"Yer got yer *own ship?*" Billy's voice held a note of awe.

"A red and blue barge!" Elissa shouted back. "I am a passenger."

Billy reached out a long arm to slow Elissa

down. "Yer can stop running, then. That's old Jarvey's barge. He left hours ago."

Elissa stopped dead in her tracks and, to Billy's obvious dismay, promptly burst into tears.

"There, there, now." Billy patted her clumsily on the head, trying to comfort her.

"They thought I was with Maya. And she probably slept straight through," sobbed Elissa. The way Maya slept, she probably wouldn't wake up until supper. Nobody would even know Elissa was gone until the barge was halfway to Gravesport.

"There's other boats," said Billy reassuringly. "And old Jarvey's an honest man. He boards with my mum portside, you see. He'll refund yer passage straightaway. Everything will be fine once yer get to Gravesport." As Billy comforted Elissa, he clucked disapprovingly and muttered something under his breath about "irresponsible mothers who slept whilst their own wee daughters were getting mugged in town" and "the sorry state the world was finding itself in these days."

Elissa, for her part, continued to sob, oblivious to Billy's awkward efforts to console her. This was a total catastrophe. She was completely alone in a strange city. How was she going to find Maya and Gertrude? How was she going to survive? All her money was aboard Captain Jarvison's barge, sewn into the hem of her cloak.

"But I don't have passage," she said hopelessly. "I can't get there."

Billy stared at the river. He scratched his head, thinking.

"Can yer cook?" he asked.

⚘ 5 ⚘

Erda's Temple

Billy trotted through the market, with Elissa close behind. She didn't want to lose sight of Billy. He was her ticket to Gravesport.

"What can yer cook?" he asked.

"Oh," said Elissa breathlessly. "Just about everything." It was true. She'd spent so long eavesdropping in the Manor kitchen that she'd absorbed most of Cook's recipes. She'd even made a few. "Stews, fried patties, savories, pastries, pies." Hers were not as good as Cook's, of course, but she could turn out a decent crust if she had to.

Billy grinned broadly. "Old Cappy's going to be happy with me this time," he said. "I did right good."

They stopped in front of a pile of orange

tubers, which Elissa examined with interest. "These look like they would make a very good stew," she said.

"Here," he said, handing her a purse.

"What is this for?" asked Elissa.

"The Captain said to give the purse to the cook. That's you," he added, just to confirm their arrangement.

Elissa opened the purse. Inside was a pile of coins—about a dozen coppers and a few silvers. She hesitated.

"What's wrong?" asked Billy.

"I have never bought food before," she said.

Billy lifted his cap and scratched his head. This was a problem that neither the Captain nor Billy had foreseen.

"Miss," he said gently. "It's not right to steal."

Elissa was genuinely shocked. Then she laughed, shaking her head slowly. "Nobody *buys* food where I'm from," she explained. "People grow what they can and trade for the rest. At home we only buy made goods—pots, pans, tools, and things like that."

Billy looked sheepishly at Elissa. "Sorry, miss," he said. "I thought—"

"Never mind," said Elissa graciously. "Just give me some pointers."

"It's easy enough," said Billy. "Yer just pay the price they ask for."

"No bargaining?" Elissa was simultaneously perplexed and relieved. Money was not something she understood very well.

"No," said Billy. "Not for food."

Elissa faced the tuber seller with far greater confidence than she had the silk merchant. By the time she was done, Billy was loaded up with a stack of sweet orange tubers and ten large starchy white tubers, which Elissa thought would be good grilled. They fit comfortably into a big rope sack that Billy had been using as a belt. The sack had the amazing quality of being able to expand endlessly. As they made their way through the market, it stretched and stretched until, along with the vegetables, it accommodated a block of brown sugar, two weights of salt, several mounds of dried fruit, four weights of flour, some leavening, a carafe of oil, and several tins of spices, which Elissa would employ to make her stews savory.

Billy hefted the sack. "Are yer finished? We

should be getting back to the boat afore too long."

"Yes, I think so," said Elissa, turning. Then she stopped, sniffing the air. "Hmm," she said. "Just one more thing." She made her way past the spice dealers to a stall from which hung rows of nondescript dried bundles.

"Perhaps we should have just a few herbs," she said. "For tea." Using her excellent nose, Elissa chose the freshest, strongest-smelling bundles of mint, chamomile, lemon balm. "For digestion," she said. She chose little bundles of comfrey and gentian in case there were wounds or illness; rosemary and other aromatics for cooking; and skullcap and valerian for headaches and general nervous states, thinking of herself more than anyone else. Then she spied a small open box filled with odd-shaped roots.

"Manroot." A shriveled old woman emerged from the interior of the stall. "You'll not find it anywhere else in the market."

Elissa looked at the manroot. Resembling its namesake, it had a knobby little head and four tapering roots coming out of the main tuber, like two arms and two legs.

"What is it good for?" asked Elissa.

The old woman winked. "Everything," she said. Then she named an exorbitant price, at which Elissa protested heartily.

"Trust me," said the old woman mysteriously. "You'll need it."

Elissa bought the smallest root. When they were finished buying provisions, Billy stopped at a cloth merchant's booth and pointed at a square of oilcloth. He asked Elissa for a copper.

"What's that for?" asked Elissa, handing him the penny. With the purchase of the manroot, the purse was nearly empty.

"For yer silk," said Billy, giving the merchant the penny and wrapping the cloth around Elissa's parcel. "The *Swamp Maiden* sometimes gets a tad damp." After he tucked in the silk, he tied the sack shut with a piece of string and hoisted it over his shoulder.

"Ready?" he asked, squinting upward. Judging from the position of the sun, they'd be able to get back before dusk.

"We have a couple of pennies left," said Elissa. She remembered the piles of exotic-looking fruit she had passed on her way to the silk quarter. "Do you think we could buy a little food for right now?"

"Anything yer want, miss," he said. "We still have some time."

Elissa tried to remember where she had seen the fruit sellers. The thought of those sweet-smelling fruits made her stomach rumble. They wound their way past stalls of hanging meat, dried fish, insects in enormous bowls—none of which Elissa could remember seeing before—until they came to a wall with a barred iron gate set into it.

"It's the inner wall to the Old City," explained Billy, who for once seemed to know where he was.

Elissa ran her hand along the smooth white wall. It was cool to the touch. Suddenly she had the urge to see what was on the other side. "Can we go in?" she asked.

Billy shifted from one foot to the other. "I don't know, miss," he said. "I've never been past the market. It's all temples and shrines in there. But I don't think there is any kind of a law against going inside."

"Well, that's good to know," said Elissa. She

pushed at the gate, which swung back easily on oiled hinges, allowing them to pass through quietly.

In contrast to the market, the Old City of Alhamazar was very quiet. The few people who passed them murmured soft greetings and then continued, shuffling their way down narrow, meandering cobble footpaths. White walls surrounded them. Tilting her head back, Elissa followed the walls as they rose up, narrowing, until they pierced the sky.

"The spires!" she cried. She hadn't meant to speak quite so loudly. Her voice sounded jarring to her own ears. "Let's just walk a bit," she said very softly. "Then we'll get a bite to eat."

Billy and Elissa proceeded down one of the winding streets. They were quite alone. There wasn't a sound apart from the dull clopping of their feet against the stone cobbles. Turning around a bend, they came upon a pleasant courtyard, in the middle of which stood a lovely tinkling fountain. Beyond the fountain, the high arched double doors of one of the temples stood open. Elissa could not resist the desire to peek inside.

"Miss," called Billy softly. "I don't know if we

can go in there." He was looking doubtfully at the elaborate doors, which seemed to Billy too fancy to admit a common sailor. Elissa was regarding the doors as well; every square inch of them was carved with plant motifs: twining vines, hanging fruits. She was reminded of the fact that she wanted a piece of fruit.

"You can go in," said a voice from the interior. "But you have to leave a gift."

Elissa, intent on studying the elaborate carvings, hadn't noticed the boy who was crouched just inside the doorway. Now she saw two bright eyes peering out from a grimy face.

"What temple is this?" she asked. The small boy scooted out from the protection of the portal. As he passed into the sunlight, Elissa realized he had been blighted at birth. One side of his body was withered. Perhaps his mother had eaten chicken bones while she was pregnant, or had had a terrible fright. She remembered that Nana always warned mothers against such dangers. She felt sorry for him.

"This is the Erdite temple," he said. "Those who worship the Earth deities come here to pay homage."

Erdites! The little girl, or wraith, or whatever she was, had mentioned them yesterday. Perhaps Elissa was meant to go in. The boy reached up and tugged on the hem of her robe.

"Buy some fruit?" he pleaded. He dragged out a small blanket on which was piled a little stack of large brown pods. Elissa had never seen anything like them—not in the market, certainly not at home. They didn't look much like fruit. Elissa's mistrust must have shown on her face, for the boy broke one open for her. The interior of the pod was filled with fluffy white wool.

"Can you eat that?" she asked.

The boy laughed and held it out to her. She took it reluctantly, watching his face carefully. He stuck out a pink tongue, whose smooth, clean surface contrasted markedly with the dirtiness of his cheeks, and made a licking gesture. Elissa imitated him. To her great delight, her tongue encountered not a dry wad of wool but a moist, delicious thread that melted instantly in her mouth, leaving behind a wonderfully sweet aftertaste, almost like the flavor of a pear, but richer.

"How much?" she asked, indicating the pile.

"Four coppers," said the boy.

"Two," said Elissa. It was all that was left in Billy's purse.

The boy pushed the pile of fruit over to Elissa, signaling that her offer had been accepted. Elissa handed him the two pennies and divided the pile in half.

"Here," she said, shoving a handful of pods into Billy's hands. She could hardly wait to finish the one she had started. She lapped up the sweet fibers with little moans of appreciation. "Delicious," she murmured between bites. The threads were wrapped around four smooth black pellets the size of peas. After she'd finished her first pod, she held one of the seeds between her fingers. It was deeply lustrous and perfectly smooth. If she hadn't known it was a seed, she would have taken it for a jet bead. She pushed the pellets into her little purse, where they clanked gently against the shard and the little vial. In short order Elissa finished off the rest of her pile of fruit, popping the seeds out of each pod and cleaning them with the hem of her robe. Between her seeds and Billy's, she would have enough to make a nice necklace. On second thought, perhaps she would plant them. *I'd love to see what kind of tree these would make,* she thought. As she felt the seeds stir against her chest, she immediately stifled the thought. *Not now!* she thought with an inward groan.

Billy rose to his feet, grasping the rope sack. "Well, miss?" he asked. Elissa cast a longing glance at the door of the temple.

"Just one little peek inside," she said.

Elissa walked to the doorway and peered through it. The boy had vanished, perhaps to some inner part of the temple. Unlike the bright courtyard, the interior was poorly lit, making it difficult to see. She could barely make out the walls and floor. Elissa took a step.

"Miss!" called Billy. "I don't know if—"

"I'm not going to stay long," she answered. She took a few more steps until she was well within the anteroom. It was dark and very quiet. It didn't appear that anyone was in attendance. Certainly there could be no harm in looking. She walked into the cool, hushed interior of the temple, placing her feet carefully so as not to create any noise. The place seemed to warrant silence.

The small, dark anteroom, where the boy had been sitting, had opened up into a large, softly lit chamber, at the center of which tinkled a fountain much like the one in the middle of the courtyard. The difference was that this fountain—in fact, the whole room—was filled with vegetation. There were plants of every variety—flowers, small bushes, clumps of grasses, vines, even trees bearing red and golden fruits. Indeed, there were so many plants that the light inside the temple was tinged a luminous pale green. Elissa advanced toward the fountain, where it seemed the flowers were clustered in the greatest abundance. As she approached it, she saw that behind the fountain was an archway— or rather an arbor, for over it crept a vine. She almost cried aloud in recognition, for from the vine hung the brown pods she had just consumed. So this was where the boy had gotten them! In front of the arch was a great pile of fruits, vegetables and tubers, bunches of leaves, baskets of grains, fragrant blossoms—all the bounty of the land. The arbor itself was carved in much the same fashion as the door but with the addition of all sorts of animals that twisted and cavorted among the twining leaves and flowers. It was like a puzzle, with birds, rabbits, deer, fish, and horses fitting cleverly among the carved plants. Upon closer look, it was hard to distinguish which figures were plants and which animals, for the artist had carved them so that they transformed themselves into one another. Elissa stared at the remarkable workmanship. The animals were so lifelike that they appeared to move.

Finally she turned her attention to the inside of the arbor. In its innermost recess stood a statue of a woman smiling upon the world, her outstretched hands filled with ripe fruit. Her head was crowned with aromatic waxy blossoms that drooped luxuriantly over her carved tresses. Piles of flowers lay at her feet. Elissa looked into the lovely marble face and experienced a sudden shock. She was staring into her own eyes! Then she realized that the eyes of the goddess were made of emeralds that caught the light and reflected it, much like Elissa's own.

Elissa stood gazing into those sparkling green eyes. It was uncanny, but somehow she had the feeling that she had come home at last. Even though she had seen no open door or window in the interior of the sanctuary, she felt the plants around her sway gently, as if they were bending before a soft summer breeze. She knew that breeze well. It was the gentle breeze of High Crossing, her own valley, ruffling the fields of barley, sighing through the apple orchards. She could smell the scent of the roses twining around Nana's door, hear the bees buzzing in the clover. At this moment it seemed that home was so close, she could reach out and touch it. And she almost did. Without thinking, she had lifted her hand toward the statue. Then she remembered that home was very far away and dropped it again. She had better go; Billy was anxious to be off.

Elissa turned and picked her way through the plants, taking great care not to overturn any as she exited. Some of the great pots looked fragile, and a few of them had already been chipped. Once she reached the anteroom, she turned for one last look at the splendid green-lit interior, one last breath of sweet highland air. However, her reverie was cut off by a hand that grabbed her roughly by her collar.

"I've been watching you," hissed an ominous

voice. "You invoked the goddess, but you didn't make an offering. All who pass before her must leave a gift."

"Oh!" cried Elissa, startled. The man who held her had thrust his face into hers. It was bright green.

"I have . . . Oh dear, I'm sorry. You see, I spent the coppers. I don't have . . . ," she stammered.

"A gift!" shouted the green-faced man. "You must leave something for the deity!"

Spying the cord around Elissa's neck, he shifted his hold and pulled at it until the little purse came out from under her blouse.

"What's this, then?" he cried, tugging at the purse.

My shard! thought Elissa, struggling in his grip. "There's no money in it!" she protested. But the man had drawn his knife, which glinted green in the dim light, and with a single cut sliced clean through the cord.

"No!" cried Elissa.

"What goes on here?" A voice rang out through the temple. It seemed to emerge from the statue of the goddess herself. The man sheathed his knife, though he still held on to her purse.

"This little urchin did not leave a gift," he proclaimed, holding aloft Elissa's purse.

A woman emerged from the arbor. For a moment Elissa thought she was the deity, for around her head she wore a crown of waxy flowers. Her robe, however, was green and flowing, not carved in stone.

"Let her go!" commanded the woman. "This is a temple, not a wrestling pit. Contributions are strictly voluntary; you know that."

Reluctantly, the man let Elissa go.

"Yes, Priestess," he said, though he did not give Elissa back her purse.

The woman approached Elissa, her arms outstretched. "Welcome," she said. "I am the High Priestess of the goddess Lyss, whose sanctuary you have entered." Elissa turned to face the woman, who suddenly and quite unexpectedly came to an abrupt halt, her face frozen in a mask of dismay.

"I was very careful," said Elissa quickly. "I didn't break anything."

The Priestess stared at Elissa with an intensity that was almost frightening. "One thousand pardons," she finally murmured. "Idiot!" she hissed to the man. "Did you not see her eyes? Have you learned nothing in this temple? Nothing at all? Now give that to me before Lyss decides to turn you into a newt!"

The woman took Elissa's purse from the trembling acolyte and ceremoniously returned it to Elissa, who examined the split cord ruefully.

"We will repair that, of course," said the Priestess, giving a meaningful nod to the green-faced man, who hurried away. "It won't take a minute to fetch a new cord."

Elissa was holding her purse in her hand. "I am sorry I didn't make an offering," Elissa said. "But I don't have any money—just a little vial and my, um, talisman . . . See?" *She will understand*, thought Elissa. *A priestess, of all people, ought to know a woman should not part with her talisman.* Elissa held her purse out over the Priestess's palm and shook it. Out spilled the mysterious broken shard she had found on the shores of the Sacred Lake, followed by a handful of shiny black pellets. In her fear of losing her shard, Elissa had completely forgotten about the seeds.

The Priestess gazed into her palm, delighted. "The seeds of the sacred fruit of the deity," she exclaimed. "This is a fine gift!"

By now the man had returned, sweaty and panting. His green face paint was dripping off in little runnels, striping his cheeks. He held out a slender cord to Elissa, who immediately threaded it through her purse.

"You have honored us with your presence, O Avatar," said the Priestess, bowing. "Please forgive us the error."

Elissa was truly confused. Her name was Elissa, not Avatar. However, she had no time to correct them. She had already stayed much longer than she had planned, and Billy must be frantic by now. She hoped he hadn't left without her; she wasn't sure she could cope with being abandoned twice on the same day.

"You have a lovely shrine," she said as she hurriedly departed.

"Thank you!" called the Priestess.

Be there, Elissa prayed as she ran down the dark hallway.

To her enormous relief, Billy was pacing around the fountain when Elissa finally emerged into the sunlight. His cap was lopsided. She imagined Billy must have scratched his head so many times that his cap would never go back to its normal position.

"Oh, miss!" he cried. "There yer be!" He grabbed the sack and threw it effortlessly over his broad shoulder. For a moment it looked as if he was considering tossing Elissa over his shoulder as well. "We'd best be cast off."

Elissa thought so, too. "Yes," she said. "This is an odd place." She glanced at the temple door. It was shut. And of the boy who had been there earlier, there was not a sign.

❧ 6 ❧

The Count

"We'll be there right soon, miss," Billy called cheerfully as he drew back on the oars.

With Elissa's assistance—she had stopped a roving honey peddler and asked for directions—they had found the dock where Billy's skiff was tied. Wasting no time, he had flung the rope bag into the bow and lifted Elissa up and over the side as if she weighed no more than a sack of milkweed. Then, grabbing the oars, he pushed them off into midriver with a single stroke. Soon they were well under way, which pleased Elissa enormously. If they continued at this speed, there was a chance she might be able to catch up with Maya and Gertrude. However, Billy traveled down the river only a few hundred yards. Once they had passed all the docks, he maneuvered the boat into a little stream that emptied into the Serena. The stream wound through some reedy marshland, until it was joined by a larger one. Billy angled the boat into the second stream. As he rowed ever farther from the Serena, the stream they were traveling upon meandered into another, and then yet another. Elissa wondered why they hadn't stayed on the river, since this seemed a very roundabout way of reaching their destination.

"The Captain's tighter than bark on a tree when it comes to paying the Wharf Master," Billy explained. "Cappy's got himself a problem with back taxes. So the Wharf Master put a watch out for him. Now if he tries to dock, they'll grab his cargo. And likely throw him in jail. So he comes the back way. The trip's a tad longer, but it's free."

Elissa thought that the length of time it took might not be the only drawback of this trip. As they moved through the marsh, she noticed that the vegetation was becoming increasingly dense. Stands of holly and laurel crowded thickly against the water's edge. Drifts of floating waterweed clung to Billy's oars. The water beneath them looked murky.

"Where are we going?" she asked.

"Swamp Landing." He glanced over his shoulder to check for low-hanging branches. "It's not much of a landing. More like a tree. Cappy'll be there, and Doc."

Elissa had no idea what Billy was talking about. The docks were back the way they'd come. And as for trees, well, there were trees as far as the eye could see, great drooping banks of them, their tangled roots hanging down into the water like wriggling masses of snakes. Elissa removed her robe. The humid air was making it cling uncomfortably to her skin. Looking up at the dense canopy of branches overhead, it was hard to imagine that not too far away was a barren desert. *It's amazing what a little moisture can do,* she thought. *A little moisture and a whole lot of plants.* Billy rowed along, but as the stream degenerated into a narrow brook, his forehead creased in puzzlement.

"I could have sworn . . ." He stopped pulling at the oars and scratched under his cap.

"What's the matter?" asked Elissa. She had the sneaking suspicion they might be lost. This did not look like the way to anywhere.

"Did you notice a white crane back aways?" he asked. "There was a white crane on the way in. Fishing. Over by the left bank, I think."

Inwardly, Elissa groaned. She fervently hoped Billy was not the ship's navigator. She had felt so relieved when Billy had offered her passage to Gravesport, but at this rate they might not even find the landing. She might never see Maya and Gertrude again. She'd be lost and alone forever. Her father would forget about her. She took a deep breath to steady herself. *I need a cup of tea,* she thought.

Billy noticed the tears in Elissa's eyes. "Don't worry, missy, I'll get us there." He shook his head, disgusted with himself. "Dolt," he mumbled under his breath. "Can't even find yer way back to the landing." With a few expert strokes, Billy brought the skiff around and rowed back the way they had just come.

"It's around here somewhere," he said. "I'll find it."

He returned to the place where the stream

had forked and took the other branch. "This'll get us there. This is the right one," he said, for his own reassurance as much as for Elissa's. However, after a quarter of an hour, they came upon another fork, at which Billy again scratched his head.

"It was right easier coming *into* town," he explained, perplexed.

"How did you do it the first time?" asked Elissa, hoping to discover some clue as to their whereabouts.

"I just followed the gulls."

Elissa looked around. The sun was sinking behind the trees. Billy looked worried.

"It'll be dusk soon," he said anxiously. "Those stingers will come out."

Elissa didn't know what "stingers" were, though she suspected from Billy's tone of voice that they weren't friendly. If Billy was worried, that was a bad sign. He didn't seem to worry about much. And Billy was right about dusk being close at hand: the moths were out. A little white one was already fluttering around her head. It hovered close to her ear. She could swear it was whispering something. The voice was so tiny, she could barely hear it, but she recognized it at once. The spirit was back.

"Left?" she said aloud.

"Yer think so?" inquired Billy. He peered ahead. "It looks just like the other one." Then he pulled them along to the left. Within a moment or two, he breathed a sigh of relief. "This is the one," he said. "I recognize that critter."

A brown rat slipped into the stream, blending instantly with the water. There was more of a current here, which Elissa imagined was a good sign. Perhaps the stream would widen soon. Elissa smiled to herself. Now that the moth was back, things were bound to go right. Perhaps it would help guide her to Maya.

Suddenly they came up hard against the shore. Elissa gasped involuntarily as they struck the bank and, turning, gasped again. There, right before her nose, was a pair of boots. Billy noticed them, too—and the legs to which they were attached. Their eyes followed the legs upward.

A young man was hanging from a pole at the water's edge. From the looks of him, he'd recently received some rough treatment. His face was marred by several bruises, and his burgundy velvet cape was torn. His outstretched hands had been bound to the long pole, which hung between two branches, leaving his feet to dangle just a few inches from the water. It looked like an extremely painful position—one that could not be endured for long. From all appearances, the young man was unconscious.

"Hold on to his legs," Billy said; he was already hacking away at the ropes with his knife. As one hand came free, he eased the young man's arm around his shoulder. "Just pull his feet over to the side there." He cut the remaining rope and slipped his other arm around the young man's chest. Then they lay him down, cushioning his head against the supplies.

"Somebody meant for him to die," said Billy as he pulled away from the shore. "If those stingers hadn't gotten him, the snakes would have."

He was about to pull into midstream when Elissa shouted, "Wait!" A glimmer from the shore had caught her eye. With one stroke, Billy returned the skiff to the bank. A sword, still sheathed in its belt, was dangling from a jagged root by the water's edge.

"Well, it looks like they left him his weapon. That was right decent of them," Billy observed.

Elissa leaned over the edge of the skiff and untangled the belt. Then she removed the sword carefully and held it up against the light. The hilt was beautifully fashioned of filigreed silver and set with precious stones. Whoever this man was, he was not a pauper. He lay with his head close to her lap. His breathing was shallow. Elissa bent over him and felt his forehead.

"He's burning up!" she cried.

"Swamp fever," said Billy. "Here, cool him off." In one swift movement, Billy grabbed Elissa's robe and dunked it into the stream. Then he handed it back to her sopping wet. Elissa draped the robe around the young man's head and neck.

"Wet his hands and feet, too," said Billy. "But not his chest."

Elissa dabbed a corner of the dripping robe along his hands and forearms, noting as she did so that he barely stirred. His face was so still, it looked carved. She twisted her head around to get a better look at him. He had aristocratic features: a high forehead; an aquiline nose, turned down slightly at the end; flared nostrils; a stubborn chin; finely etched lips. Even in repose it was a proud face, stamped with the mark of authority. Elissa was reminded of her father. He might have looked like this when he was young. She peered down at the youth, wondering what color his eyes were. Would they be dark, like her father's? From the deep black of his hair and the tone of his skin, she guessed they were brown.

Billy rowed with all his might, skimming along the ever-widening stream like a waterbird in flight. They were approaching a narrow peninsula. As Billy drew up to the far side, Elissa could see a dock jutting directly out from the base of a tree, the likes of which she had never seen before. Its enormous trunk covered half the width of the peninsula, and its thick branches stuck straight out from its sides, like arms. A ladder ran up the trunk. As Elissa stared, she could just make out what looked like a cabin nestled among the branches.

"Swamp Landing!" announced Billy. "We're back!"

"And it's about time, too! Where have yer been? The moon?" A burly man with a full salt-and-pepper beard was clambering down the side of the tree. For all his girth, he was as nimble as a squirrel. As he neared the boat, his eyes flashed in anger.

"Bucko, ya dolt! What have yer brought me? A child and a dead man! Have ye no sense at all?" The bearded man snatched his cap from his head and used it to flail Billy about the head and neck.

"Yer a disgrace to yer mither!" he howled.

"I got us back, Captain," wailed Billy. "Besides, she can cook—and *he* ain't dead . . . yet."

"But the *Count* will be dead soon if we don't help him," interjected Elissa in her firmest voice. The big man with the beard didn't look as if he was ready to listen, but the young man at her feet wouldn't last long if she didn't act. Of course she had only the foggiest notion of what a count might look like—after all, she had been dead wrong about Falk—but she believed a noble title would impress the Captain. At the very least, it would shift his attention away from Billy, who didn't need any help, and onto the young man, who did. As it happened, she was correct.

" 'Count,' did you say?" The burly captain stopped swatting Billy and cocked an interested eyebrow at Elissa. Elissa handed him the sword, which he fingered thoughtfully.

"Nice work," he observed, handing it back. Then he leaned forward into the boat to take a long look at the young man. "Doc'll fix him up," he said. He crooked a forefinger at Billy. "Come along, Bucko. Make yerself useful."

Billy lifted the young man out of the boat and draped him over his shoulder. "I'll bring the supplies up the back way, Cappy," he said, seeming to take no offense at his previous treatment. The Captain stood aside to allow Billy up the ladder. Then he climbed up after him.

The ladder didn't look strong enough to hold all three of them, so Elissa waited until the Captain had passed out of sight before she slung the sword belt around her shoulder and put her foot on the first rung. Adjusting the belt with one hand and grasping each narrow rung with the other, she made rather unsteady progress. The sword clanked against her hip at each step, slowing her further. By the time she passed through the cabin's low doorway, Billy had disappeared. Elissa entered the room and immediately began to cough. The cabin was filled with smoke, and it was so dimly lit that she could hardly see. She peered through the haze, her eyes watering.

In the center of the room was a pallet, upon which lay the young man. Next to him crouched a monkey, which Elissa found interesting. She had never met a monkey before, but Nana had told her stories about them. They had always struck her as intelligent animals, with their inquisitive natures and dexterous fingers—just like a person's, Nana had said. Elissa couldn't be sure, but it appeared to her that right now the monkey was doing something distinctly human with his fingers; he was taking the young man's pulse. Elissa lifted a hand to rub the tears from her eyes. There was so much smoke! As she drew closer, she was disappointed to see that the monkey was actually a small, grizzled man. He looked at her intently with bright eyes and then turned back to the Captain, who was positioned on the other side of the pallet. The old man murmured something to the Captain, who shook his head slowly. The situation looked grave.

"Can ye make some tea?" asked the Captain. "Doc here says he needs hot liquid." Without taking his eyes off the young man, he pointed to the back of the room.

Elissa headed directly to the rear of the structure, toward a small opening through which smoke entered in great drifts. *Where there is smoke,* she said to herself, *there is fire.* When she had passed through the low door at the back of the cabin, she immediately spotted a brazier burning away on an open porch—just as she had suspected. A stick of green wood had been placed across it, creating the foul, vaguely familiar-smelling billows of smoke Elissa had smelled when she had first entered the room. Even outdoors, the smoke made her eyes sting. *What kind of people burn green wood?* she wondered. *Any child knows it doesn't make a good fire.* She removed the branch and took a deep breath of fresh air.

Elissa looked around for a rain barrel and a pot. Both were located under the eaves, near the brazier, as was the sack of provisions. *Either Billy has wings,* she thought, *or I am moving slower than a slug in molasses.* She filled the pot with sweet water from the barrel and then rummaged around in the sack of provisions. In short order she found the bundles of herbs she'd bought from the old woman. She grabbed the manroot, and using the razor-sharp edge of the sword, she cut off its head.

"Sorry about that," she apologized. Somehow it looked pathetic with just its thin arms and legs sticking out. The head, however, was the strongest part—at least that was what Nana had always said about plants—so she meant to use it first. She scraped the sides of the little knob to remove the grime, chopped it into three pieces (Nana had always told her that three was a charm), and placed them into the pot.

Boil roots, steep leaves, Nana had taught her. But how long should she boil the manroot? Elissa decided to keep the pot going until the liquid was half gone. The young man was going to need a strong infusion. While she waited for the water to boil, she busied herself peering into the various crocks and barrels on the porch. One of the crocks held a salt cod in water in which, from the looks of it, it had been soaking for quite a long time. Another contained what looked like the beginnings of a soup. A few pieces of something pale floated around a greasy wooden ladle that had been left in the pot. Hesitantly, she sniffed at the broth, then lifted the ladle to her lips.

"Ugh," she said. She moved the pot onto the brazier and withdrew one of the tubers from the sack.

"I'll bet this is the fanciest cooking knife in history," she said as she peeled the tuber and cut it into bite-sized pieces with the young man's bejeweled sword, which was sharper than a razor. In another bag she found black-spotted peas. She threw two or three handfuls into the broth. Next she rummaged around in the sack until she found her seasonings.

"Aha!" she said. "These ought to do the trick." She threw a pinch of pepper into the broth. She added coriander, cumin, and some rosemary for extra flavor, then tasted the broth again. "Mmmm . . . ," she murmured approvingly. "Much better." Soon the stew was bubbling merrily in its clay pot.

Elissa checked the manroot infusion. The liquid was a deep, strong brown. It was ready. She searched around for a cup, finally locating one amidst some broken crockery. The edge was badly chipped and it was filthy, but it would have to do. Wiping out the inside with the hem of her shift, she filled it half full, then blew on the surface of the liquid until it cooled. As she was turning to reenter the room, a spark from the coals flew up and burned her on the forearm. *I'll attend to that later*, she thought.

She walked into the room slowly, holding the cup with both hands. She didn't want to spill a drop of the precious liquid. Besides, the floor of the room was tilting at a crazy angle, making each step precarious. Elissa was uncomfortably aware that she hadn't eaten very much that day. Her head felt light. She approached the pallet where the young man lay. The old man was still crouched beside him. Fortunately, the loud captain was gone. She didn't want to have to deal with him.

At Elissa's approach, the old man looked up. "Save that tea for someone else," he said in a subdued voice. "I am afraid it's too late for this poor lad."

Elissa put down the cup of tea and peered into the young man's face. His eyes had sunken into dark pockets, and his nostrils had the pinched look of imminent death. But he was not yet gone.

"Lift him up," she said. The old man obeyed her command without question. When the youth had been raised to a sitting position, Elissa tilted his head back, resting it against the old man's arm.

"Open his mouth," she said, drawing her little purse out of her blouse by its new cord. While the old man reached around with his other hand and lowered the young man's jaw, Elissa removed the stopper of her silver vial and pressed it into her palm, envisioning Sohar as she dripped the water of the Sacred Lake into Maya's parched mouth. Elissa squeezed her eyes shut for a moment. *You saved Maya,* she prayed. *Now save this young man.*

Once his lips had parted, Elissa poured in a few drops. Then she waited for the swallow reflex, but the liquid dribbled out of his mouth. She poured a little more of the water between his lips, massaging his throat to stimulate the muscles. This time she felt the liquid go down. She repeated this procedure until the vial was nearly empty. Then the old man carefully laid the youth back down.

Elissa waited. She didn't know what she was waiting for. Perhaps she was waiting for a "Sign," like Mama Red Flag. It might be her imagination, but the young man's eyes already appeared a little less sunken. She absently massaged the spot where the spark had burned her. It itched horribly. She held still, barely breathing in her concentration. The room was as silent as a tomb. Elissa wanted desperately to lie down, but still she watched. She couldn't rest until she was sure he was out of danger.

Some color was returning to the youth's face. The old man smiled at her in relief. For a brief, scrambled moment, Elissa was sorry he hadn't turned out to be a monkey. She'd have liked to have had the opportunity to chat with a simian. Perhaps some other time. Elissa scratched again at her arm. It was beginning to burn. Then she shifted her gaze back to the young man. For some reason, once she looked down, she was unable to take her eyes off him.

Suddenly his eyes opened. He looked Elissa full in the face and spoke a single word.

Elissa gazed into his eyes. They were the darkest she had ever seen—black, like the color of a starless night. His eyes grew larger, filling first his face, and then the room, until their darkness closed in all about her. His brief utterance echoed in her mind as she tumbled helplessly into the midnight sky.

"Lyss . . ."

7

A Good Tale of Betrayal, Murder, and Revenge

It was still dark. Elissa wondered what had woken her up so early. Perhaps one of the cocks had crowed. It was probably that little bantam, out to impress the hens. *The smaller the cock, the louder the racket,* she thought. Elissa yawned and stretched. She might as well get up. Nana would be needing her to start the fire and get breakfast ready. Then there would be herbs to gather, bubbling pots to monitor, Gertrude to feed.

"Doc!" a voice called. "She's waking up!"

Doc? Elissa tried to sit up, but a large hand pressed her gently back. "Where—"

"Not yet, miss. Wait till Doc gets here." Elissa looked up into a concerned freckled face that did not belong to anybody in High Crossing. Then, all in a rush, her memory came back to her. She lay back down. There was no point asking where she was; Billy Buck probably wouldn't be able to tell her.

"What happened?" she inquired.

A grizzly-haired man appeared at Billy's side— Doc. Now she remembered. He was carrying a cup. Doc gestured for Billy to help Elissa sit up.

"You might still feel a little weak, but this will restore you. Drink up." He held the cup out to Elissa but didn't let go of it until he was sure she had a good grip on it. Her right arm felt a little wobbly.

Elissa took a sip and nearly gagged. "What's *in* this?"

Doc chuckled. "Touch of your own medicine, plus a dollop of mine."

Reluctantly, Elissa took another sip.

"Drink up," said Doc.

Elissa held her nose and downed the contents of the cup. To her relief, she soon felt considerably revived.

"Thought you might like to see this." The man held out his hand. Across his palm lay a short, rusty needle. "I took this out of your arm. I noticed you were scratching it. So when you passed out, I went back to the stove and found you'd taken off the smoker."

Elissa was puzzled.

"The smoke from the camphor stick keeps the stingers away," he explained.

Camphor! She thought the smoke smelled familiar! Nana always used a camphor rub for coughs. As for the needle, Elissa remembered that Billy had mentioned something about stingers, but she couldn't remember the context. Her head still felt fuzzy.

"How long was I out?"

"A night and a day."

Elissa pushed herself upright.

"I've seen worse," said Doc. "You only got the one sting. It's a good thing there was some of your medicine left. Manroot tea." He nodded appreciatively. "When it comes to teas, you sure know what you're doing." He fixed his bright eyes on Elissa. "What was in that vial, anyway?"

Doc cocked a furry eyebrow at her, but Elissa didn't answer. She had lost a whole day. Maya and Gertrude would be well on their way to Gravesport by now. How would she ever catch up?

While Doc waited patiently for Elissa to answer, a tall figure appeared next to him.

"The Count has been keeping steady watch over you." Doc inclined his head toward the dark young man. "He insisted."

"The Count?" Elissa shook her head, befuddled. Doc must mean that young man they'd rescued yesterday. Or was it the day before? But how could he have kept watch over her? The last time she'd seen him, he was nearly dead.

"Count Favian of Leonne, at your service." The young man made a short, stiff bow, his cape flaring behind him theatrically.

Elissa almost laughed. So he was a count after all! It seemed she had a knack for identifying nobility. Maybe she had more of her father in her than she thought. The dark-eyed young man had, in fact, made a rapid recovery. His bruises had faded almost completely. Elissa felt for her little purse and patted it gratefully.

The Count was looking down at Elissa, which made her feel a bit uncomfortable, as she was sitting, quite literally, at his feet. It wasn't an admiring look he gave her, or even a pleased one.

In fact, it reminded Elissa of the sort of look she might give her soup if she found something strange floating in it. Then, without warning, he drew his sword from its sheath and presented it to her.

"I owe you my life, fair maiden. Therefore, in the name of my mother, the Countess Rowenna, and my father, Count Beltran of Leonne, and all my mother's fathers and father's fathers and those who passed before them for seven generations, I pledge my sword and my honor . . ." He paused to take a breath and cast a quick glance at his spectators.

Doc and Billy looked impressed, which seemed to satisfy him. But Elissa couldn't stifle a grin. No one had ever called her a "fair maiden" before, and what was this about mother's father's fathers?

Seven generations, she thought. What would she do with them all? For some reason, she found the idea enormously funny. Elissa hiccuped.

Ignoring her, Favian continued his oath of fealty, ". . . until thine enemies be smitten and the debt be repaid—"

"I have no enemies to smite," interrupted

Elissa, trying very hard not to giggle. "However, I do appreciate the kind offer. You can put the sword away now."

The young count held himself stock-still for a moment. His eyes blazed. Elissa didn't need an interpreter to read that expression: *How dare you refuse my offer to maim and kill other men for you!* It was obvious she'd offended him. But in spite of his flashing eyes and the sword in his hand, she didn't feel intimidated. "Speaking of smiting," she said, "who tried to kill you?"

Favian gave her a withering look, and for a moment Elissa thought he was going to smite *her* for sheer impertinence. What was wrong with her? She *knew* it wasn't proper to ask personal questions of nobles. It must be the residual effects of the manroot—or perhaps it was Doc's "dollop."

"My brothers," he said.

Now he had her attention, as well as the interest of everyone else in the room, which had undoubtedly been his intent. He raised his eyebrows—a silent request to tell his story. Elissa waved her hand, graciously indicating that he had her permission to tell his tale.

"Thank you, *my lady*," he said, making no effort to temper his sarcasm. Elissa smiled sweetly.

Favian began his tale with a flourish.

"I am the rightful Count of Leonne, wrongly accused, judged, exiled, and then foully betrayed." The young count's audience settled in, relishing the dramatic opening.

"Pass the hardtack," Billy whispered to Doc.

"As you all probably know, my father, the Count of Leonne, is recently deceased," Favian announced. He looked around the room, expecting signs of recognition on the part of his audience. Much to his disappointment, Billy continued to munch away, while Elissa merely shook her head. Only Doc nodded.

"Well," muttered Favian under his breath. "At least one person in this shack keeps up with the news."

Doc turned to the group. "Leonne is the strongest, and largest, of the Western holdings," he explained. "Somewhat similar to the position Castlemar holds in the east. Right now it is suffering from a power vacuum."

Elissa nodded thoughtfully. She had learned something of politics from her experience with Falk.

And if Leonne was anything like Castlemar, Favian's relatives were not to be trusted. But he probably already knew that.

Doc shrugged apologetically at the Count, who was tapping his foot. "Didn't mean to interrupt."

"That's fine." The young man cleared his throat and continued with his tale. "My father had three wives, who bore him five legitimate sons. There may have been others as well, but they don't count."

"How can children *not count*?" asked Elissa, incredulous.

Favian curled his lips into a condescending smile. "It is customary for men in my father's position to have mistresses. Indeed, bearing the child of a high noble is considered a privilege."

Elissa hmphed, which seemed to irritate Favian. He turned toward Billy and Doc and continued.

Elissa examined Favian closely. He was more than a little pompous. She was sorely tempted to tell him that he'd offered to defend her honor with the same sword she had used to dice turnips, just to see how he would react. Still, she had to admit the young noble intrigued her. What piqued her interest was not his quaint manner but his eyes. They periodically flashed with tiny red sparks. Though his face never moved a muscle, not even a telltale hardening of his jaw, she knew he was angry—no, furious. She wondered how he managed to keep all that fury contained.

"My father's first wife, Ileana, bore him two sons, Armand and Reynaud. Ileana hailed from one of the far Western holdings, I don't know which. My father never spoke of her. Apparently she was frail, for she died when Armand and Reynaud were very young. After her death, my father married my mother, who also came from the West. Her name was Rowenna of Abela. I was her only son. I lost her when I was a mere child, five years of age. My father returned home from riding one day and told me she was dead. An accident—or so he said."

Favian's tone of voice alerted Elissa. She knew the deep pain of betrayal, and she recognized it in Favian. It must have been awful for him to be suddenly left without a mother.

As a child, he couldn't have been able to understand.

"It's hard to believe," Elissa said, speaking her thought aloud.

Favian clutched his sword, and for a moment it looked as if he might lose his iron composure. "I found it hard to believe him myself," he said. "She was an excellent rider." He took a deep breath and continued his tale.

"Scarcely a month after my mother's death, my father married Sonia of Arania. She was heiress to some sizable lands on our southern boundary and was very rich. However, though she was young and extremely beautiful—"

Billy's eyes brightened. "Fair or dark?" he asked.

Favian cast Billy an unreadable glance. "Fair," he said curtly. "She was also devious, underhanded, and treacherous. My father, unfortunately, always turned a blind eye to her character, if not to her wealth. His holdings were greatly expanded through the union. She bore him twins, Avaro and Ludo—my younger brothers." Favian corrected himself. "Half brothers. The spitting image of our father, Beltran. Red-faced brutes, the pair of them. Thank the gods I take after my mother." Absentmindedly, he touched his dark hair.

"A year ago, after a long illness, my father died, leaving Armand, his firstborn, to run his domain. Within a month, Armand was killed in a border skirmish with some desert raiders. Reynaud, the second in line, assumed his position. A few weeks later, he, too, was killed, in a similar incident. The raiders were never identified or captured. With Armand and Reynaud gone, I was next in line. On the day I was to have been named Count—my eighteenth birthday, in fact— my younger half brothers appeared at the ceremony to contest my title. They entered the hall carrying my sword, which was covered with blood, and they told the whole court that the blood belonged to Reynaud. And to compound the lie, they produced a supposed witness, a poor half-witted serf, who said that a masked assailant had killed my brother with this, my very own sword."

He held up his sword for effect. Billy was

entranced. "Those sailants are *everywhere*," he whispered to Doc. "This is some line o' work Cappy's gotten me into."

Doc looked baffled.

"How did that sailant murder yer brother with yer sword?" Billy asked.

"He didn't," said Favian. "I was wearing the sword the day my brother was killed. But on the day I was to be named Count, I was required to wear my father's sword for the ceremony. I had to leave mine in my quarters. It was easy for my brothers to sneak into my private chambers. All the guards had been assigned to the main hall. They killed a calf or a sheep, I imagine, in order to present a bloody sword before the court."

"Didn't anybody notice that the blood was fresh?" asked Doc.

"They noticed, all right," said Favian grimly. "But not one of them was willing to step forward and defend my honor. They were too afraid. By then Sonia was the true ruler of Leonne. For years she had been spinning her web of power, strand by strand, as my father declined slowly in health and vigor. None dared oppose her."

Some spiders eat their mates, thought Elissa.

"I left the hall in disgrace. That same day I was escorted to the border by my half brothers. They allowed me nothing save this sword"—Favian held up the glinting steel—"and the clothes on my back. It was fortunate for me that my uncle, Theo, insisted on accompanying us. If he hadn't been there—"

Doc nodded sagely. "Curtains for you, my boy," he said.

"Unfortunately, Uncle Theo could do but little. However, there was something I could do. I walked ten paces"—Favian took a few steps away from the group and whirled around, making Billy gasp—"and then I turned to face my brothers as they sat upon their steeds. 'The gods watch, and the gods listen,' I cried. 'A curse upon your house for the injustice I have suffered at your hands. You shall die without heirs—both of you.' I turned my back to them and strode away, knowing that as I walked their eyes were trained upon me in hatred."

Favian paused dramatically. There was utter silence in the room.

"From that day on, I have traveled on foot,

hiring myself out as a private soldier to local landlords—for land disputes, that sort of thing. I was heading for the market at Alhamazar, where I hoped to enlist some mercenaries to help me regain my title. But before I reached the city I was accosted, beaten unconscious, and dragged off to die in the swamps . . ." He glanced briefly at Elissa. "Where you found me."

"Gaw, that's a right mean town," observed Billy.

"My half brothers arranged the attack, of course," said Favian. "The fact that I still have my sword proves it."

His audience looked perplexed.

"In Leonne it is bad luck to take the weapon of a murdered man," he explained. "The fact that my sword was not stolen proves that those who attacked me were my own people. Anyone else would have taken it." He held the sword before them and tilted it so that the jewels embedded in the hilt caught the candlelight. The constellations of tiny red garnets glinted dangerously in their filigreed silver nests, giving back the glow of the fire. But the single large ruby dominating the center seemed to contain a fire of its own. The weapon was clearly one of a kind, made by a swordsmith who had surpassed himself in its creation. But for Favian, its true worth lay elsewhere.

"It was my mother's," said Favian quietly. "Presented to me on the day she died, by my uncle, as was her wish. One day, I shall seek justice with it." Favian glanced down at Elissa. Her brilliant green eyes were not fixed upon the glittering sword, as were all other eyes in the room, but focused fully upon his face. Abruptly he sheathed the sword, which made a faint soughing sound as it slid home.

Doc and Billy breathed a joint sigh of contentment. There was nothing like a good tale of betrayal, murder, and revenge to finish off the day. The Captain, who was just then climbing up the ladder, entered the room to find his crew in a state of bliss. He scratched his head under his cap and lumbered back to the porch. Shortly afterward he reappeared with a steaming bowl in his beefy hand. He plunged his spoon into it.

"The *Maidie*'s shipshape and ready to go," he announced to the silent group. "Yer dern quiet. What have yer been up to?" he inquired between enormous bites. When nobody answered, he briefly stopped gulping. Then, almost as an afterthought, the Captain waved his dripping spoon in Elissa's direction.

"By the way," he said, "yer hired."

8

The Swamp Maiden

The next morning, after Elissa had eaten her fill of sweet, sticky porridge, she followed Billy down the ladder and through a stand of dense bracken to the other side of the peninsula, where the *Swamp Maiden* was docked. As soon as Elissa set eyes on the ship, she knew it would sink before it reached Gravesport.

"Welcome aboard the *Maidie!*" bellowed the Captain.

"The gods help me," murmured Elissa. She walked up the gangplank leading to the bottom deck in total disbelief. *This isn't a boat,* she thought. *It's a disaster.*

The *Maiden* looked like something that had been cobbled together out of parts intended for something else. Indeed, when Elissa looked more closely, she saw that it had been. The deck railings looked like they came from several different and completely unrelated structures. Some had been turned in fancy spirals, while others had remained rough-cut. Mismatched spindles had been joined to the rails in no particular pattern. Occasionally one was missing, creating a gap-toothed effect. Every few yards, one of the posts supporting the second deck stuck up aimlessly, like a maypole waiting to be danced around. Chipped remains of paint in all different colors adorned the deck boards and sides. As Elissa lifted her eyes to the second deck, she thought she saw the scalloped edge of a lace curtain.

The boat itself was roughly oval, with what looked like two bows, one fore and one aft. It had a flat bottom joined to slightly curved sides just high enough to keep out the slosh of river water. The second deck hovered over the bottom deck on stiltlike posts. Like the bottom deck, it was open, except that a small, flat-roofed cabin was cupped in its slightly sagging middle. Doc and Favian had already climbed to the second deck, where they were stretching an awning from the cabin roof and coiling great loops of rope. The uppermost deck, which was perched on top of the cabin like a little hat, merely held two chairs.

Elissa assumed that the oddly shaped bladders attached to either side of the ship were meant to keep it afloat. She peered over the side, examining their construction—skins of some kind stretched over ribbed frames. From above, they looked very much like strange headless, legless animals with great bloated bellies. It was clear they'd been in the water a long time. Delicate aquatic plants were growing on them, trailing out into the water and up the sides of the boat like long green hair.

In fact, some *were* hair. A woman's long tresses had been painted onto the sides of the boat. Elissa moved to the rear, following the flowing green lines until they met the head of a lovely maiden—the Swamp Maiden herself. Elissa leaned over the back of the boat to look into the face of the figurehead. Her gilt had almost completely flaked off and part of her nose was missing, but her eyes were large and farseeing as she gazed upriver. Elissa wondered what she was doing at the back of the boat. Weren't figureheads usually at the front?

"Aye, my *Maidie* will get us there. Never fear," called the Captain. "She's never been beached, nor sunk, nor becalmed."

Elissa could understand why the *Maiden* had never been becalmed. The boat had no sails to hang empty. In fact, it looked as if the only way to get her to move at all was through the combined efforts of three men wielding poles. Wisely, Elissa kept her opinion to herself. By rights, a captain needed to possess a certain amount of pride in his vessel. He might need to go down with her. In this case, he probably already had—more than once.

"Come on up," he said, pointing to a rickety ladder. Elissa held her skirts up as she fastidiously stepped around the damp piles of rope and rusty tools that lay scattered about the bottom deck. She passed Billy, who was loading a number of heavy-looking burlap sacks into some bins, and climbed up to the second deck. Doc, the Captain, and Favian were conferring, the ice apparently having been broken between them.

"The galley is all ready for you," said Doc, waving his pipe toward the front of the ship.

Elissa followed Doc. When the boat sank, she

observed, at least she'd be higher up. That would give her a little more time to think about what to do.

As Doc had said, the galley was indeed "ready." Under the awning were stacks of cups and bowls, assorted clay vessels with handles and spouts, and an open sack from which the tips of stirring spoons, knives, and other kitchen implements emerged. On the open deck, a row of copper pots was lined up next to a flimsy four-legged brazier, upon which sat a large iron kettle. A fire was already smoking.

"If this thing tips over," Elissa remarked, "the whole boat will go up like a torch."

Doc chuckled. "She's got too much rot in her to burn," he said. "You'll be hanging your hammock right here." He pointed to a support pillar, from which hung a sagging mass of tangled rope. Elissa couldn't imagine how she was going to sleep in such a thing until Doc pointed to a hook set into the side of the cabin.

"You'll sleep like a babe," he said, noting her expression.

Curious, Elissa poked her head into the cabin, wondering what the Captain's quarters looked like. But instead of a bed, she saw bins filled with food supplies, fishing gear, and netting. Lanterns hung from the rafters, along with coils of rope, slings, and various tools whose purpose Elissa could not guess. Oddly, a set of rough shelves at the front held a stack of books, a red petticoat, and, most incongruous of all, a basket of silk flowers. She spotted her oilcloth-wrapped packet tucked beside them.

"You'll find everything you need in the storeroom," said Doc.

"Apparently," murmured Elissa.

They pushed off. Much to Elissa's amazement, the *Maiden* did not immediately sink. In fact, as the craft floated smoothly through the swampy waterways, she began to understand the reason for its unconventional construction. The shallow draft of its flat bottom allowed it to glide over the underwater hazards of wetlands travel—the sharp tips of submerged branches, creeping roots, mudbanks, and masses of floating waterweed. And if the boat did get snagged, it was easy to swing it around in a circle. Billy and Doc would simply take up their poles and move from one end of the boat to the other—which, in any event, were nearly identical. The *Maiden* was an ungainly-looking form of transportation, but no more so than Ralph, Elissa concluded.

Elissa set to work sorting supplies, peeling, chopping, mixing. As long as her hands were busy, her mind remained idle. But when her hands were idle, she felt the insistent tug of impatience. She was anxious to be reunited with Maya and Gertrude, of course. But now that she had time alone, she realized she was just as anxious to be reunited with Falk. Going back over all their encounters in her mind, she wondered if she had interpreted his actions correctly. That time in the woods, when they were playing Five Questions, had he meant to crush the moth, or had he meant to caress her cheek? And he'd been saying he'd rather have an honorable defeat than an ignoble victory when she and Gertrude had found him in the Blue People's encampment. But she'd focused solely on his calling her a "bargaining chip." Hadn't he been expressing regret just then? There were so many signs that she had missed, so many alternative explanations. But she wouldn't know the truth until she saw Falk again, face to face. When would that be?

But there was no way to hurry the *Maidie* along. As the days wore on, Elissa told herself she had no choice but to accept the delay, and she set about to perform her duties to the best of her abilities—much to the joy of the crew, who devoured her succulent fritters, crispy fried bread, and savory stews with relish. Cook had taught her well, even if she hadn't intended to. After a while, Elissa began to enjoy the relaxed pace and easy drift of the *Maiden.* The swamp had its own particular allure. There was a tantalizing element of mystery to the hidden flow of its waters, the jungle vegetation that crowded along the river-bank. Like the desert, the swamp was reluctant to yield its secrets to the casual observer.

The growth was so dense that one could see only a little way into the jungle, but sometimes Elissa caught moving shapes that appeared and disappeared among the shrubs that crowded the shadowy banks. At night, as she lay under the netting that kept biting insects at bay, she listened to the soft rustling of jungle animals moving through the trees. It was amazing how many creatures inhabited the banks along the river. Their murmurings, calls, and occasional sharp cries filled the night with a steady, deafening chorus. She could not help but follow their talk, though they kept their communications short and to the point: *Be careful; I'm coming; All clear; Stay away!* Wild animals don't waste words. For many of them, a lengthy chat could cost them their lives. Elissa tried hard to keep her ears open, listening for new voices above the din. Oddly enough, the more she listened, the less she heard. A sort of low, continuous hum blunted even the most strident of calls. At first Elissa had thought she was hearing a different species of animal. But lately she'd begun to think she was listening to something else entirely. No animal she knew could produce such a deep, soothing hum. When she tuned in to it at night, it lulled her to sleep. That and the sweet, heavy air.

The air here was as densely packed with odors as the jungle was with animals. There was one intensely penetrating scent that filled Elissa's nostrils just as the sun was setting. Every evening, while she was doing her chores, she breathed in the sweet perfume hungrily.

Doc found Elissa leaning over the side of the boat one evening, trying to catch a glimpse of the fragrant bloom. "Don't lean over too far," he joked, "or we'll all go under."

"What's that smell?" Elissa waved vaguely toward the riverbank. "The one that comes every evening."

"It's called 'Smells at Night.' "

"What kind of a name is that?" asked Elissa.

"It's a translation," explained Doc, removing his pipe. "The people who used to live here named everything like that." He pointed to some skunk cabbage. " 'Plant That Stinks.' " He pointed to a tree with a shiny trunk that glowed faintly green in the reflected light of the moon. " 'Smooth Bark Tree.' "

"What did they call the river?" asked Elissa.

" 'Lots of Water,' " said Doc. Somehow Elissa was not surprised.

Elissa peered into a stand of tall, straight trees, their swollen bases half submerged in the brackish water. She tried to imagine what it must be like to live among them.

"The jungle people called those trees *topilwa*," said Doc, pointing to them with his pipe. " 'Swamp Tree.' The honeybees love them."

"What happened to the jungle people?" asked Elissa. "Are they still here?"

"Maybe," said Doc. "But it's been a while since I've seen any. They called themselves the Iyuri."

Elissa waited expectantly.

"Meaning 'People.' "

Doc made a soft drumming sound against the side of the boat with his fingers while Elissa continued to search the banks for her elusive flower. She wondered aloud how she would recognize it.

"You'll know it when you see it," said Doc.

Elissa accepted Doc's word on that. Every afternoon, when the sun began to sink, Elissa eagerly awaited twilight, wondering if tonight would be the night. In the South, dusk is not drawn out, as it is in the North. The day vanishes so quickly that, in a moment of inattention, night can take one unawares. And Elissa had so many chores: the fire had to be lit, a stick of camphor placed on the embers, the soup set to boil, and the mosquito netting arranged over her hammock well before the sun started to disappear behind the trees.

One late afternoon, when the treetops loomed dark against the slowly fading sky and the bats emerged for their nightly dance, wildly swooping and darting over the river, Elissa abandoned her fire, taking up her post at the side of the *Maiden*. She narrowed her eyes, focusing on the play of shadow against shadow. *How could people live in there?* she wondered. The brush growing along the shore was so dense, she couldn't imagine anybody being able to pass through it. Then, all at once, she saw a flash of white. A moment later, the air was filled with the heavy, sweet scent of the flower. Then the flash was gone. But shortly afterward, another flash appeared, then still another, each one leaving its haunting aroma behind as a reminder of something beautiful yet unattainable.

"Found 'em, did you?" asked Doc. He had come up silently behind her, watching her as she inhaled appreciatively.

Elissa smiled. "I was looking for them too late in the day," she said. Now that she knew where—and, more important, *when*—to look, the flowers were easy to spot. Their waxy petals shone like miniature lanterns against the gigantic blackened leaves of the umbrella-like plants that grew close behind them. It was as if each plant sheltered a tiny candle at its center. But the flower's light was cool, unlike the light that flashed in Favian's eyes.

The young count had not spoken much to Elissa since telling his sad tale. He had willingly, and ably, participated in the handling of the boat, much to the astonishment of everyone on board. He wielded his pole as if he'd done this kind of work all his life, bailing tirelessly and enthusiastically sharing the crew's jokes and meals. Although he appeared to work well with the crew, it seemed to Elissa that he was avoiding her. When she served supper, he took his bowl, thanking her politely, but he kept his eyes shuttered. Yet even though he maintained his distance, she sometimes caught him staring at her while she cooked. Once, when their eyes had met, he started forward as if to speak with her. But then he must have changed his mind, for he said nothing and busied himself elsewhere. Tonight Favian was nowhere to be seen.

"Some people call it Flower of Lyss," said

Doc, abruptly bringing Elissa back from her contemplation of Favian.

Elissa remembered where she had seen the waxy blossoms before.

"I saw them in the Erdite temple!" she exclaimed.

Doc nodded. "Yes, they are Erda's favorite," he said. "And very difficult to obtain, so they make an especially good gift."

Elissa thought for a moment. The priestess had said she served Lyss, not Erda. She told Doc about her experience in the temple.

Doc listened with his brow furrowed, thoughtfully puffing on his pipe.

"She called me Avatar," said Elissa. "Who is that?"

Doc put his pipe down. "An avatar isn't really a 'who.' It's more like a 'what.' "

Elissa looked confused.

"You see, Erda doesn't have a body, as we do. She's the spirit of the Earth, so we can't see her. But when she takes on physical form, we call that an avatar. The Erdites worship three avatars, which to us look like ordinary women—one young, one mature, and one old. But they are really goddesses."

Doc cast a sidelong glance at Elissa. She appeared to be lost in thought.

Doc cleared his throat.

Elissa turned her luminous eyes toward him, and Doc caught his breath. "The Erdites believe that sometimes, when we are in grave danger, Erda walks among us," he said carefully, "in the form of Lyss, the green-eyed girl."

"Oh," said Elissa. "Then that's probably why they mistook me for her." Elissa shook her head. She didn't understand gods and goddesses very well, but she knew that there was great danger in the world. It had been predicted. "The end of the world is near," Om Chai had said. Maybe Doc would be able to explain the prophecy, although he was looking at her rather strangely tonight.

"Do you think the world is going to end soon?" she asked. "I mean, there are droughts where I come from. And other places, too, I've heard."

Doc pursed his lips. "Here as well," he said. "Every year, the swamp gets a little smaller." He studied his pipe. "Everything is in balance," he said. "Water, earth . . . When the rains don't come, the land fails, and then people begin to fight."

"Do you think that is how it will end? In war?" Elissa asked. She thought of the desert, of farms giving way to sand and ruins, of the earth drying up. "Or in drought?"

Doc looked into Elissa's eyes and answered honestly. "Neither one. Wars have always been with us, as have droughts. No, in the end, I think it will be greed that does us in. People will do anything for gold, even if it means destroying one another. They'll even destroy themselves. They'll destroy the whole world if they think it will make them richer than the next man."

Elissa frowned. "But there is enough for everyone," she observed. "It seems foolish."

"Aye, that it is," agreed Doc. "But such foolishness is the way of the world, eh?" He gazed at her, as if for confirmation—or guidance.

Elissa looked into the jungle, heard the beasts calling to one another. They might hunt one another, eat one another, but they would never destroy themselves and everything around them for a few shiny trinkets. A flash of white appeared at the water's edge—one of the blossoms had fallen. It drifted slowly toward the *Maiden*. As Elissa peered down into the water, it turned over, and as it turned the petals transformed themselves into an old-fashioned white dress. Elissa found herself gazing into a pair of round, bright eyes. Then, with a smile and a little wave, the ghost of the Serena was gone.

"Not my world," said Elissa.

Elissa stirred the pot. It would be time for supper soon, and she was making a stew. But her mind wasn't on her work. They had been traveling now for six days. Tomorrow they would make their landing at Gravesport, and her first task would be to find her friends. Elissa was worried that Maya and Gertrude would be gone by the time she arrived. After all, they had no way of knowing what had happened to her; she'd been on the *Maiden* for nearly a week. Even if they were still there, how would she locate them? Gravesport was a huge city. Perhaps the Captain would help her find a schedule of departures at the Dock Authority. He was gruff but, as it turned out, kindly. His bark might be loud, but his bite was nonexistent. Sort of like Bruno's old dog Cassius.

But then again, perhaps the Captain was not

on speaking terms with the authorities in Gravesport. He probably wasn't on speaking terms with authorities anywhere. Elissa absentmindedly fished a pretty yellow snake out of the stew. Snakes were attracted to the bright copper of the pots and kept flinging themselves into them from overhanging branches. She frowned as she threw the snake into the water. There must be manor houses or offices of some sort where she could inquire.

"Most girls would have screamed."

Elissa screeched involuntarily. "Favian! You surprised me!"

Favian shook his head ruefully. "Apparently I am more loathsome than a snake," he said. "They might be poisonous, you know."

"They won't bite me." Elissa realized her tone had been overly confident, but she had no intention of explaining to Favian why snakes wouldn't injure her. Favian was looking at her quizzically. "The soup shocks them," she said quickly.

"Nevertheless, fear of snakes is universal. I have also noticed that you don't seem—"

"Do you know the Lord of Gravesport?" Elissa interjected. She didn't know what Favian had noticed about her, but it was bound to be something not to his liking.

Favian hesitated, his brow furrowed in thought. "There is no lord," he answered.

Elissa looked puzzled. "No lord?" she asked. "Then who rules the city?"

"Gravesport is run by a city council, usually elders who are appointed by the different guilds," he explained. "They make all of Gravesport's laws and regulations."

"Could I speak with them?" Elissa's voice was tremulous with hope.

"It would take weeks to get an appointment! Why? Do you have a law you want passed?" He chuckled.

Weeks! She didn't have weeks to find Maya and Gertrude. "Then who is in charge of daily affairs?" she asked.

"That would be the Sheriff of Gravesport. He is an old friend of the family—a former noble in my father's court." Favian's mouth tightened. "My stepmother exiled him as well."

Elissa's eyes brightened. "Do you think he could help me locate someone? Someone who arrived by barge?"

"Of course he could," Favian said with confidence. "I will make sure of it. He keeps the trade registry. The name of anyone entering or leaving the town on business is recorded there."

"Why, there must be dozens!" exclaimed Elissa.

Favian gave Elissa an indulgent smile. "Hundreds," he corrected. "But the Wharf Master also keeps a registry, as does each innkeeper. The Sheriff collects the lists every night. That serves to control contraband." He was curious to know who Elissa was searching for, who could make her eyes shine so brightly. And even though, as a noble, he needn't bother asking permission to inquire, he felt compelled to.

"If I may be so bold," he began, "I notice you are traveling alone, and in . . . unusual circumstances. May I ask whom you are seeking? Family? A suitor, perhaps?"

"Gertrude, she's a donkey, and—"

Favian drew himself up with offended dignity.

"Ah, yes, a donkey, of course," he said sarcastically. "I am sure the Sheriff would be simply delighted to assist you." Then, with a click of his heels, he withdrew.

Elissa shook her head. He hadn't even let her finish telling him about Gertrude and Maya before his eyes had flashed red again. For the life of her, she could not figure out what she had said to provoke him. She heard a thin shriek—"Banzai!"— and stepped aside. "Silly snake," she said as she pushed it overboard with her toe. Half the time they didn't even make it into the pot.

∽ 9 ∝

"I'm Called Shadow"

Elissa awoke to the sounds of shouting. Sleepily, she swung her feet over the edge of her hammock and immediately fell down. Something was terribly wrong with her sense of balance or with the boat. She drew herself upright, using a support post. Indeed, the deck was canted steeply. Grasping the support posts one at a time, she wove her way around the deck to the ladder, which she carefully descended toward the source of the commotion.

"Dolt! Ye've run us aground!" The Captain's face was red from shouting.

"It weren't my fault!" protested Billy.

"Weren't yer fault?" bellowed the Captain. He snatched his cap from his head and stomped on it in a rage. "Then who was it poled us into this mess?"

"I was following the wee fishies," said Billy, pointing helplessly at the blank surface of the river.

Wee fishies!" The Captain advanced menacingly, hands outstretched. "Well, yer can right well join them!" It wasn't clear to Elissa whether the Captain meant to heave Billy overboard or strangle him. Perhaps he hadn't decided yet.

Doc and Favian appeared, drawn to the noise.

"What's happening?" asked Favian, yawning. Elissa noticed that he avoided her eyes.

Doc stared over the deck rail into a mass of tangled roots. "Looks like a bladder's been punctured. It'll have to be drained and patched."

"Blast! We'll be set back a day!" cried the Captain. "Maybe two! No thanks to Master Dolt here!" Arms flailing wildly, he whacked at Billy, who held up both hands ineffectually against the onslaught.

Doc cocked an eye at Elissa. "Can you make a bit of tea?" He jerked his thumb expressively toward the Captain. "Calm him down a bit."

Elissa climbed back up to the second deck to start a fire. Fortunately, the coals hadn't spilled from the brazier. They were still hot from the previous night and needed only a little coaxing to flare. She shoved two pieces of broken crockery under the brazier's legs to keep it level and set the kettle to boil. Within minutes the water was bubbling. She threw some valerian, chamomile, and lemon balm into a clay pot and poured the boiling water over the mound. Then she tossed a cup of oats into a copper pot and mixed them with some water from a jug. While the breakfast porridge cooked, she sniffed at the steeping brew and added a generous pinch of skullcap. *This would slow down a charging bull,* she thought, straining the golden liquid into a cup.

As Elissa had suspected, once the Captain had drunk some tea and wolfed down a bowl of porridge, he was able to reassess the situation with a measure of calm. "We'll still be hard-pressed, but it's a good thing we've got a couple of extra hands," the Captain said. He nodded to Favian. "Count, after breakfast, ye and the Dolt prop up the starboard side and get to draining the bladder." Without so much as a glance at Elissa, Favian followed Billy down to the lower deck to fetch poles, ropes, and pry bars.

"Hmph," snorted Elissa, watching him disappear down the ladder. She tossed her head and turned away.

The Captain was still issuing orders. "Doc, go ashore and tap a milk tree for a patch. We'll need a fair amount, with all the damage Billy's done."

Elissa regarded Doc enviously. She knew she was going to end up doing something like boiling, chopping, or grating. Milking a tree sounded much more interesting than food preparation. Besides, she was dying to see the jungle. "Can I go with Doc?" she asked.

The Captain shook his head. "The jungle is dangerous, lass. There's all manner of beasts lurking in there."

Elissa nodded enthusiastically. *Exactly.* And what wouldn't she give to chat with some of them! "I can help carry the milk," she said. Doc had emptied some potatoes from a large basket and was placing three tin buckets, some odd tongue-shaped tubes, and a length of twine inside it.

The Captain looked at Doc, weighing practicality against caution. "Can yer use the help?" he asked.

Doc nodded his gray head. "I could use a pair

of deft hands and a strong back," he said. "I'm not as young as I used to be."

The Captain snorted. "*Ye* were never young. Take her, but mind she doesn't get into trouble. It will be a sad day for the *Swamp Maiden* if our cook ends up as somebody else's supper." As Elissa happily trotted off behind Doc, the Captain called, "Wear high boots! For snakes!"

At Doc's request, Elissa packed a loaf of flatbread, a jug of cider, and some dried fruits. She sawed off a hunk of dried fish for Doc and put it in the bottom of the basket, far from the other food. It had the consistency of leather and, judging from the smell, probably tasted a good deal worse, but Doc, Billy, and the Captain seemed to enjoy chewing on it. Favian, perhaps wisely, always found something else to eat.

It was going to be a chore getting off the boat, with the side tilted up at such an angle. Doc threw the basket down to Billy, who was waiting on the shore, and then, grasping the edge of the rail, swung to the ground. Elissa looked over the side of the boat dubiously. It was quite a drop, and the tangled nest of roots that had snagged the *Maiden* looked sharp.

"Just jump," said Billy, waving his arms. "I'll catch yer."

Elissa held her breath and stepped over the rail.

"There yer go, miss," said Billy, setting Elissa down. "Yer lighter than one o' Cappy's sacks." He immediately turned back to the task at hand, which was to prop up the *Maiden* in order to raise the leaking bladder out of the water.

"We'll go through the break there," said Doc, pointing away from the river and toward the dark jungle. Elissa couldn't see anything that looked like a break—just trees and more trees. Doc bent over and searched along the bank until he found two long, smooth sticks lodged among the roots. "You'll need this," he said, handing her one of them. "So you don't fall into any holes, and for mud." Doc demonstrated how to test the area around the roots. "I'll go first, in case we run into anything dangerous." He brandished his walking stick in the air.

Elissa lifted the basket and shifted it around to her back, adjusting the strap around her forehead. "What are we looking for?" she asked as they set off.

"A tree with smooth bark and shiny leaves," Doc said. "We'll find it once we leave the shore. Watch your step!" Doc nimbly leapt over an exposed root thick enough to qualify as a tree trunk. "And don't step in the mud!" he cried. "Or you'll lose those boots!"

Elissa thought she might lose the knee-high boots anyway, as they were at least a couple of sizes too large. She picked her way carefully through the masses of roots, poking her stick into spots that looked soft. She didn't want to trip, especially with the basket on her back. Occasionally the stick sank deep into a pocket of mud, which she avoided by walking in Doc's footsteps. Most of the time, he seemed to know exactly where to step without looking. She concentrated on her feet.

"Here!" called Doc. For a bowlegged old man, he had managed to get quite a distance ahead of her. He waited while Elissa caught up. "It will be easier now that we are going uphill. We are almost past the mangroves."

Doc was right. Ahead of them, the jungle floor was remarkably clear. Doc pointed up as he walked. "It's the canopy," he said. "It filters out so much light that smaller plants can't survive. So there's no underbrush."

Elissa eased the strap away from her forehead with both hands and looked up. Above her, the tops of the trees leaned their leafy heads together to make a green roof. She couldn't see any direct sunlight at all, but the whole jungle glowed with a diffuse light, which filtered down through the straight trunks of the trees like pale green liquid. It was disappointingly quiet.

"Where are the animals?" she asked, looking around. "The Captain said there were beasts."

"Don't worry," said Doc. "We're making enough ruckus to warn them off. Besides, it's early yet. The deadliest of the carnivores won't come out until dusk."

"Which ones would those be?" asked Elissa.

"The Iyuri called them *yaguas*," Doc said. " 'Kills in One Leap.' " He made a hooking gesture in the air behind his head with two bent fingers. "They can take a man's head right off."

As they walked up into the jungle, Elissa wondered what a *yagua* might look like. She imagined that to take a man's head off, it would need to have large fangs, like a wolf. Or perhaps it was some sort of bird, with an immense beak and sharp talons. Nothing was more powerful than an eagle or more deadly than a hawk. But neither bird slept by day, and neither could remove a head. Cats, on the other hand, hunted mostly at night. But cats were not fearsome animals—except to mice.

Once again Doc called. Elissa trotted to catch up, her hands cupping the bottom of the basket in an attempt to keep it from jouncing. By the time Elissa reached Doc, she was somewhat winded.

"This is it." Doc patted the wide trunk of a tree that rose straight up into the air. Elissa put down her basket and stick and craned her neck, attempting to see the top, which was impossible. The tree must have been a hundred feet tall. Then she examined the trunk. It was completely smooth. She walked around it.

"What are you looking for?" asked Doc, removing a short-bladed knife from his pocket.

"Well," said Elissa, putting her hand on the smooth trunk. "I see we've brought buckets. But if we are going to milk it, where are the teats?"

Doc laughed so hard, he had to lean against the tree. "That's good," he said, wiping his eyes with his sleeve. "I'll have to remember that one." Doc placed the knife's blade against the bark of the tree at about chest height and, piercing the thin bark, drew the knife down in a diagonal spiral around the tree. Elissa gasped.

Doc stopped in midcut. "What's wrong?" he asked.

Elissa had sat down, holding a hand against her ribs. "Stitch in my side," she said. "It will pass."

"Rub it," said Doc. He finished scoring the tree and then gouged a second cut, at an angle alongside the first, to make a narrow channel while Elissa rubbed her pain away. Then he rummaged in the basket, found one of the odd tongue-shaped tubes, and, with the hilt of the knife, banged it into the tree at the end of the cut he'd made. He adjusted it so that it tilted downward. White liquid was already seeping down the channel. He placed a bucket beneath the tube.

"Are you recovered?" he asked gently. "Can you help me tie this to the trunk?"

Elissa nodded and rose to her feet. Her side

felt better, but there was still a bit of surface pain. She took the length of twine from the basket and wrapped it tightly around the bucket and tree trunk. Then she cut the end with Doc's knife. The white liquid slowly dripped down the tube and into the bucket.

"This is going to take a long time," said Elissa.

"That's why we have three buckets," said Doc. He had already started walking. Elissa picked up the basket and followed at a short distance, hanging back to allow Doc to locate another tree and make the diagonal cut before she arrived.

When Elissa reached the tree Doc had chosen, she watched him work, pressing a hand against her side just in case. But this time there was no pain. Elissa took out a tube and fastened the second bucket, her mind busy.

She closed her eyes for a moment, recapturing the earlier event. She realized that she had been touching the first tree as Doc cut into the bark.

Doc signaled her to follow him and they headed deeper into the jungle, looking for yet another tree. Soon Doc stopped again. This time

Elissa deliberately held her hand on the trunk as Doc made his slash. She squeezed her eyes shut. As soon as she felt the pain, she dropped her hand, stifling a gasp. Doc stopped working.

"Another stitch?" Doc peered at her from under his bushy eyebrows, his eyes bright.

Elissa nodded. *This is bad,* she thought. *I'll never be able to prune Nana's apple trees again.* But once she removed her hand, the pain ebbed away. She tied the bucket to the tree, frowning. "Will this *harm* the tree?" she asked.

Doc looked at Elissa curiously. "No," he said. "It's a very shallow cut, see?" He pointed at the narrow gash. "And the milk fixes the wound. It's no more than a scratch."

"Good," said Elissa. She was happy that the tree would not be permanently injured, but she remained thoughtful.

"How about some lunch?" asked Doc, gesturing toward the basket. "It will take a few hours for the milk to collect, and this is as good a place to eat as any."

Elissa readily agreed. The walk had made her hungry. She removed the flatbread and jug of cider and handed them to Doc, who politely broke off a piece of bread for her before eating his own. Then she passed him his chunk of dried fish and some leathery fruits. They chewed in companionable silence, appreciating the peace of the jungle around them. When they were done, Doc stretched out on his back.

"Time for a nap," he said. "Billy interrupted my beauty sleep this morning with his expert navigation." He put his cap over his face and crossed his arms over his chest.

Elissa lay back as well. She wasn't sleepy, but she wanted to think a bit. She had felt Doc cut the tree, which could only mean one thing: the waters of the Sacred Lake of the Ankaa had enhanced her Gift. No, not enhanced—they had *changed* it. First the waters had enabled her to talk to plants, then they had made it possible for the plants to know what she thought, and now, it seemed, she could *feel* what they felt. She never knew plants could feel pain before. She wondered if she would ever be able to pick a flower or harvest a vegetable again. Then something else occurred to her. *If plants can feel pain, what else can they feel? Pleasure, love . . . anger?*

Her thoughts were interrupted by a movement

overhead. High above them, the branches swayed and rocked. It was hard to see with the sun behind the leaves, but it looked as if an animal was jumping from branch to branch. Then it came into view—inquisitive face, hands like a person's. *It looks like Doc,* thought Elissa. *It must be a monkey.*

She sat up and looked at Doc, who by this time was snoring. *He'll be asleep for a while,* she thought. *Surely it won't matter if I take a little walk.*

Elissa rose and, brushing the bits of fallen leaves and dirt from her skirts, started walking in the general direction the monkey had taken. After a step or two, she slipped out of her clumsy boots. There was really no need for them here. Once she had achieved a little distance from Doc, she looked up to check for movement in the branches. She cupped her hands around her mouth. "Hallooo," she called, not too loudly. "Anybody up there?"

There was no answer, just raucous laughter. A moment later, an object came hurtling down through the branches and exploded at her feet. The smell of sugar rose to Elissa's nostrils. She leaned over and dipped her finger into the red and golden mess, then placed it in her mouth. Delicious!

"Hallooo," she called again. This time she was prepared and caught the fruit before it struck the ground. "Thank you," she called. Once again there was no answer, just more laughter. *Well, the joke is on them,* she thought. *I'm getting free food.* She bit into the ripe fruit. The flesh was luxuriantly smooth and sweet, tasting somewhat like a cross between a strawberry and a peach. She'd have to ask Doc what it was called. Probably "Tastes Good" or something like that. As she walked, it occurred to Elissa that she should return before she got lost, but up ahead she could see some strong, unfiltered light. Perhaps it was a clearing. She walked toward the light.

"Go away!"

The voice was unmistakably annoyed and curiously muffled, as if it were coming from inside a cave. Elissa looked up, but there was no movement in the trees. Nothing was hurled at her. She stepped into the light.

Elissa was surprised to see an enormous tortoise in the center of the clearing, its legs and head retracted into its shell. The tortoise had been maneuvering its way around the trunk of a fallen tree, whose collapse had provided this little island of direct sunlight.

"Leave me alone!" rumbled the tortoise. So this was the source of the voice. The question was, Who was the tortoise addressing? A moment later the mystery was solved.

"Got you!" A large, stocky black cat leapt from behind the fallen tree and onto the tortoise. It was clear from the scratch marks on the tortoise's shell that the cat had performed this trick several times already.

"Stop that at once!" cried the tortoise, cautiously extending her neck.

The cat batted at the tortoise's head, which she quickly retracted. "Miserable creature!" the tortoise cried, her voice resonating hollowly. Then she extended her two front legs, rapidly tilting the front of her shell upward. The cat scrabbled for purchase but in the end helplessly slid off onto his rump, with a surprised look on his face.

Elissa could not help but burst into laughter.

The cat scowled. "Don't make fun of me," he growled. "I am a mighty hunter."

"Oh," said Elissa, gasping. "I'm sure you can outrun any tortoise."

The cat stood up with dignity and, stiff-legged, marched toward the surrounding jungle.

Elissa immediately relented. "Don't go!" she cried. It would be a pity if the only animal willing to talk to her stalked off in a huff. "I'm sorry!"

The cat turned and faced Elissa, then approached her. As the cat drew closer, Elissa saw that although he was large, he was not full-grown. His fur was still a bit fuzzy, like a kitten's, and his ears and paws looked too large for his body.

"I'm Elissa," she said. She crouched down and held her hand out for the cat to sniff.

"I'm called Shadow," said the cat, disdaining her outstretched hand. Elissa patted the cat instead, then automatically scratched him behind his ears, just as she had scratched Willie hundreds of times.

"Ahhhh." Shadow lowered himself to the ground, his eyes closing ecstatically. "A little down, a little back. Ahhh . . ."

Elissa smiled. A cat was a cat. They liked their

comforts. Shadow stretched toward her hand and purred, a deep rumbling sound that made the ground vibrate.

Then, at the sound of a whistle, Shadow stopped purring. His body stiffened.

Suddenly a scream tore through the peaceful fabric of the jungle. "What's *that*?" asked Elissa.

"*That's* Mama," said Shadow.

An immense black form separated itself from the trees. This was undoubtedly the biggest cat Elissa had ever seen or ever would see; it was at least the size of a man. Her claws, extending from her paws, were a good five inches long, and when she roared, her fangs looked as if they could pierce armor. The cat's long tail twitched, as if she were preparing to leap.

"Mama!" called Elissa. "Your son is fine!"

The cat paused. Slowly, she padded across the clearing.

"Shadow! I told you not to go wandering off," she said, nuzzling her son and licking his face with a long pink tongue.

"Yes, Mama," said Shadow, wincing. "I know. Don't do that, Mama."

"Who is your . . . little friend?" asked the cat,

turning her great head and fixing glowing yellow eyes the size of goose eggs upon Elissa.

"That's Elissa," said Shadow.

"I am Night," said the cat. "Thank you for finding my son."

"I wasn't lost, Mama!" protested Shadow. "I was hunting."

Suppressing a smile, Elissa pointed at the tortoise, who was wending her deliberate way across the clearing.

Night cuffed Shadow soundly. "That's not food!" she said. "I've told you, that's an Old One. My apologies!" she called to the tortoise.

"What is the younger generation coming to?" said the tortoise, turning her head slowly and leveling a cold, unblinking stare at them. "There is simply no respect anymore!"

As the tortoise lumbered away, Night turned her attention back to Shadow. "Come along," she said. "It will be dusk soon, and we have some real hunting ahead of us."

"Dusk?" asked Elissa. "So soon?" She had been walking longer than she thought. Perhaps Doc had awakened and was wondering where she was. She should get back.

Night raised her head gracefully and flared her nostrils, sniffing the air. "It is time to go," she said.

Elissa watched Night walk away, her shape flowing as smoothly and sinuously across the clearing as a dark river. Shadow followed behind, leaping and batting at insects. Elissa rose to her feet hurriedly. If it was almost dusk, the stingers might be out.

As Elissa moved under the trees, she noticed that it was considerably darker, although that might simply have been the effect of leaving the clearing. Fortunately, the path she had taken was not difficult to retrace. She found the smashed fruit, now covered with tiny flies. She felt one of them land on her arm. But when she looked down, she saw it wasn't a fly after all; it was a needle with wings—a stinger!

"Don't you *dare* sting me," warned Elissa. "I was very ill last time."

The insect rose from her arm. It flew close to her face, circling her head. "Sorry," said a voice so tiny that Elissa had to hold her breath to hear it. "I'll tell the others you aren't food." Then it flew away.

Elissa was shocked. Since when did insects speak? The only insect who had ever communicated with her had been the little moth, and there was considerable doubt in Elissa's mind as to whether the moth actually was an insect, as it certainly didn't act like one. Elissa was beginning to realize that much more had changed in her than she had originally suspected. *If only Maya were here,* she thought. *She'd help me figure things out.* But on second thought, maybe not. Maya rarely spent her energy thinking things through. Still, it would be a relief to talk to her.

Soon the wide smooth trunk of the milk tree appeared in the filmy light. Doc was just rousing himself.

"Did you sleep well?" asked Elissa, pulling on her boots.

"Like a babe," said Doc, stretching. He rose and looked into the bucket. "Ah," he said with satisfaction. He worked the tube free and began to untie the bucket.

Elissa peered over his shoulder. "It doesn't look like much," she said.

"It's enough," said Doc.

Elissa carefully placed the bucket into the

basket. The milky liquid, she noticed, seemed to have thickened into strings. She hoisted the basket onto her back and followed Doc to the next tree, where, as she pried the tube loose, she thought she felt a little shudder of relief go up the tree. Doc untied the bucket.

Soon the basket held all three buckets and they were ready to return to the boat.

"Is it too heavy for you?" asked Doc.

Elissa flexed her knees and bounced. "No," she said. "It's not much heavier than before."

"Good," said Doc. Picking up his stick, he began walking back in the direction of the river. As they approached the mangrove swamp, Elissa felt whirring wings pass close.

"And don't bite *him*, either," she whispered. The insects flew away, and Elissa marveled. Not only did they speak, they paid attention.

The treetops swayed softly overhead, and the odors of the jungle—spicy, dense, pungent with rot and new growth—rose with each step. Elissa breathed the complex perfume deeply into her lungs, grateful for the greenish light, and the sweet fruit, and the grace and beauty of the dark shapes moving through the trees. Farther along,

Doc walked serenely down the trail. A glimmer of reflected light shone through the trees ahead. They were nearly at the river. There was a question she wanted to ask Doc before they reached the boat and were overwhelmed by chores.

"Doc," called Elissa. "What do *yaguas* look like?"

Poking his stick into the ground before him, Doc answered without turning.

"Big cats."

∞ 10 ∞

A Bad Business

By the time Elissa and Doc returned to the boat, there wasn't much daylight left. The birds had started their evening calls, and a stick of camphor was smoking on the brazier. Elissa immediately began preparing a soup for supper while Doc and the Captain discussed repairs.

"We can get a coat or two on tonight," said Doc. "But the bladder won't be ready until tomorrow."

The Captain blew out a short, violent gust of air. "Well, there's no help for it," he said. "Let's get to work."

While Billy and Favian dragged the punctured bladder onto the deck where the brazier was already smoking, Doc placed the buckets of congealed milk directly on the coals. As soon as the metal warmed, the gooey strings turned back into liquid. After fetching a large curved needle and some thick clear thread from the supply cabinet, Doc sat down to work.

Removed from its frame, the bladder looked like a huge fish without insides. Although it had spent the afternoon drying in the sun, its underside, which had rested in the water, was still a slimy green. It smelled rank. Doc didn't seem to mind. He draped the formless mess over his knees as he inspected the damage.

"One small tear," he announced optimistically. He set to work sewing, humming tunelessly under his breath. When he had cut the extra thread with his knife, he held up his handiwork.

"Ye'd make someone a good wife," said the Captain. He was holding a bucket in one hand and a brush in the other.

"Is that a proposal?" asked Doc, batting his eyes.

The Captain guffawed. "Naw, yer right ugly! I've seen hyenas with prettier snouts than yers!"

They set about painting the milky substance over the tear. When they were done, they dried it over the smoking camphor, which turned the white patch dark. It gave off an unpleasant sour smell.

"Two more coats ought to do it," said Doc. "We'll be shipshape tomorrow."

"Good," said the Captain quietly. "The sooner we get those sacks off my *Maidie,* the better."

That evening, the Captain took his supper on the top deck. Normally, at the end of the day he busied himself by shouting at Billy, but the lad had already gotten an earful. Tonight Cappy was in the mood to sit and puff on his pipe. The Captain leaned back in his chair and drew in the sweet smoke.

"A drop of tea, Cappy?" Doc was waving a cup at him from the second deck. With the way the day had gone, it was hard to refuse one of Elissa's brews.

"Perhaps just a wee tad," he said.

Doc made his way slowly up to the Captain, careful not to spill any of the liquid. He handed the cup of tea to the Captain and sat in the chair beside him.

"Aye, Doc. M'thanks." The Captain sipped loudly. "I'll be sleeping with the angels tonight. I don't know how she does it, but that 'Lissa makes a concoction that lies like a mother's hand on a babe's fevered brow."

"Aye, she does," agreed Doc. "And I'd give my eyeteeth to know how she does it. Not to mention what's in that little vial of hers."

"Ye'd look right peculiar without yer teeth," remarked the Captain mildly. "How was it out there today?"

"It was easy going," said Doc. "There was almost no mud." Doc pushed his cap back, recollecting. "That Elissa. She took to the jungle like a native. You'd think she'd been born there. There's something about her—"

"No mud, eh?" The Captain drank some more tea, distracted.

Doc fell silent. He turned to face the Captain. "What ails ye, Cap?"

"I'm thinking this may be my last run," said the Captain.

Doc peered at him from under bristly eyebrows. "Is it those sacks? You've been touchy ever since Billy loaded them."

"That's part of it," he said.

"What do you think is in them?"

"Don't know, and I don't want to know. The terms were no questions asked. So I'm not asking. They'll be off my hands tomorrow." The Captain rubbed his forehead, as if trying to erase his thoughts. "What will we do with ourselves, Doc? You've been swamping long enough to see the changes."

Doc looked past the dark line of the shore to where the jungle lay, quietly shrinking. "There's always the sea," he said.

The Captain made a strangled sound through his beard. "I hate waves. All that heaving and hoing. It makes my stomach lurch just to think about it. Not to mention pirates," he said.

Doc nodded. "More of 'em every day, too, circling outside the ports like sharks smelling blood."

"They're a shameless lot," said the Captain. "Lily tells me some of them have taken to selling their own 'pirate insurance' right on the docks. Of course that doesn't guarantee safe passage from all the other brigands on the high seas." He paused, drawing on his pipe. "Tomorrow we'll be docking at the landing. When we do, I want yer to take the Count and the little miss straight into town. See that they are stowed away at Lily's. Then come back for the unloading."

Doc cocked an inquiring eyebrow at the Captain.

"It's a bad business, this cargo, I feel it in my bones. The fewer people involved, the better." The Captain drew on his pipe again. "Better still, have Billy take 'Lissa and the Count. My sister will never forgive me if any harm comes to her dolt of a son. We'll drop them all off at the island. Billy can take them to Gravesport in the dinghy, and then it'll be just you and me."

"And what if harm comes to *us*?" asked Doc.

The Captain clapped a heavy hand on Doc's shoulder.

"Old swamp dogs like us?" he laughed. "We can handle anything."

The next day, the *Swamp Maiden*, her bladders once again slimily intact, set off at sunrise. Elissa nearly burned the gruel she was cooking, for her mind was elsewhere. Soon they would be docking at Gravesport. If what Favian said was true, she should be able to locate Maya and Gertrude through the Dock Authority—which she intended to do *without* Favian's help. Perhaps Doc would come with her, just to make sure everything went smoothly.

At noon they pulled up alongside a small island, on which stood a single rickety shack.

"What's happening?" Elissa asked. "I thought we were going to Gravesport."

Billy shrugged. "Cappy wants to land us here. It's near enough to home." He was holding a coil of rope and a bailing bucket in his hands.

"Home?" Elissa was confused.

"Me mum lives portside," Billy said proudly. "I'm to take yer and the Count to my place."

"Hurry up, Billy, you clod!" shouted the Captain. "We've not got all day."

As Billy tossed the rope and the bucket onto the shore, Elissa clambered down the gangplank. Favian followed close behind. Elissa felt uncomfortable in Favian's company. His aloofness had grown since their last conversation. And for all her eagerness to find Gertrude and Maya, this was entirely too abrupt an end to their journey. She barely had time to wave goodbye to the Captain and Doc before they drew in the plank.

Almost immediately the Captain disappeared among the cargo bins, looking preoccupied. Before he took up his pole, Doc leaned his grizzled head over the side and stretched out his hand.

"All the gods be with you!" he exclaimed. Then he pulled his hand back in surprise. Elissa had pressed her little silver vial into it.

"There's only a drop or two left," she said.

Doc's eyes shone as he gazed down at the vial. "I'll never forget you!" he called as they drifted away on the current.

As the *Maiden* swung around the bend and out of view, Favian watched in silence, his brow deeply furrowed.

"Let's shove off, Count!" Billy had dragged a small dinghy from the shack and pushed it into the water. While Favian steadied the boat, Billy threw the rope and bucket into the bottom and, with his sleeve, brushed off spaces for Favian at the bow and Elissa at the stern.

As he took his place, Favian put an uneasy hand on the hilt of his sword. Elissa caught the glint of the ruby's fire, and though Favian did not give voice to his thoughts, she thought she understood the troubled look in his eyes. There was a disquieting note of finality in Doc's parting words.

Billy rowed with great vigor, and as he pulled the oars he sang, *"Oh, the life of the sea for me, for me. The life of the sea for me."*

11

The Black Cylinder

Billy sat in the center of the dinghy, cradling the oars in the crooks of his elbows. He had stopped rowing to scratch his head. "Now, where is that little birdie?" he said. "It must be around here someplace."

"I knew it," Elissa muttered under her breath. After rowing downriver for a while, Billy maneuvered the dinghy into the shallows of the swamp. "I know a shortcut," he had said. But at this point they had been in the boat for hours, rowing down one murky little stream after another until, one by one, they had petered out into dried mudflats. Elissa was sure they had passed the same hollowed-out log at least three or four times. For the life of her, she could not understand how Billy's mind functioned. He seemed to have no working knowledge of north, south, east, or west. Nor did he seem to have any comprehension of the value of fixed landmarks. The day was waning, and Elissa felt taut with frustration. She spied a gull perched on a half-submerged branch. It didn't look too intelligent, but at any rate it had to be more knowledgeable than their current navigator. *Desperate times call for desperate measures,* she thought.

Elissa took a deep breath and threw caution to the winds. "Which way to Gravesport?" she called.

Cocking his head in Elissa's direction, the bird hopped up the branch. "Come along," cried the gull, taking flight.

"Follow that bird!" Elissa commanded.

"Righto," said Billy, taking up the oars. "That's the one. Didn't I tell yer?"

Elissa thought it was a very good thing that Billy's powers of observation were limited to creatures. He seemed to notice very little about people, which made it easy to hide her Gift. Elissa guessed that she could probably have had a full conversation with that gull and Billy would have been none the wiser. And Favian, if he even noticed, would only think that she was mad. As it was, he looked down his aristocratic nose at her every time she opened her mouth. How she missed sweet little Maya . . . And oh, what she wouldn't give for a nice long talk with sensible Gertrude.

Favian rolled his eyes. "Peasants," he groaned.

Once they'd abandoned Billy's "shortcut" and returned to the Serena, Billy rowed so hard that the dinghy practically flew across the water—although Elissa nearly groaned out loud when they passed the little island where they had docked earlier that day. In spite of the good time they were now making, a twinge of anxiety ran down Elissa's spine. The sun was sinking low. Already the water was turning opaque and the birds were calling their first good-nights. Where was the town? Elissa felt distinctly relieved when she spotted a faint light twinkling ahead of them.

"We must be getting close to Gravesport," she said, pointing toward the shore. But even as she pointed, she realized the light could not be coming from a dwelling. There was only one light, and it was moving.

Favian drew his sword. "Hush," he whispered.

He put a hand on Billy's shoulder to stop him from rowing. For a moment the three of them sat still, watching the riverbank.

The light bobbed among the reeds by the shore. As the boat drifted in silence, they heard voices. Favian gestured toward the riverbank, and Billy swung around without a splash. They wedged the dinghy into a mass of gnarled roots.

"You wait here," Favian whispered. Then he climbed up onto the roots and disappeared into the dim jungle.

All was quiet. Somewhere in the thicket, a bird chirped. Elissa and Billy looked at one another.

"I hate waiting," said Elissa.

Billy nodded.

They kept close to the riverbank, skirting tree trunks and hopping over half-submerged branches and roots. After a few moments, the dense vegetation gave way to a grassy landing. Billy and Elissa crouched behind a fallen tree trunk.

In the center of the clearing stood two robed figures, their hoods pulled low over their faces. In the fading light, their robes appeared to be black.

Although they did not move or speak, there was an air of menace about them. Opposite the two men stood the Captain, holding a lantern, with Doc by his side. They didn't look happy.

"I know we're late, but we've delivered yer cargo," said the Captain. He motioned toward a pile of sacks that lay near the shore. "Now, where is our pay?"

One of the men said something. At this distance, the hood muffled the man's words, but the Captain's reply came through loud and belligerent. "What do yer mean by 'later'? We agreed to payment on delivery," he bellowed. "That means now. And yer can tell yer master we'll not be making any more shipments for him. Terms is terms."

What happened next was hard for Elissa to fathom. The hooded man raised his hand. Suddenly there was a flash and a bang. Instantly the Captain cried out and collapsed. As Doc reached foward to catch him, the second man toppled Doc with a blow to the back of his head. Billy began to rise, but Elissa quickly grasped his arm. "Not yet," she hissed. Where was Favian?

The man who had raised his hand drew back his hood. He had a hard, lean face, all angles and sharp points.

"Well, what do you know?" he said, holding up what looked like a black stick. "This thing really works. Do you think I should use it on him, too?" He nudged Doc with his foot.

"No," said the other. The second man's face was still hooded, but his voice had a peculiar flatness that made it distinctive. "We'll drown them instead. Between the eels and the fish, there won't be a trace of them left by morning. You take the feet." The two men bent over, taking Doc's limp body in their arms.

At that moment, a loud crash came from the other side of the clearing, followed by a thrashing sound. The men dropped Doc instantly. The one whose face was still hidden motioned for the other man to be quiet. Then they both made their way cautiously toward the source of the noise.

"Go now," whispered Elissa. Billy rose to his feet and noiselessly made his way through the trees in the direction of the thrashing, which was doubtless caused by Favian. No jungle animal would make that kind of commotion. A moment later Elissa heard a shout, abruptly cut off by the sounds of blows and heavy thuds—then there was a silence, signaling that Favian's work was done. Elissa could wait no longer. By the time Billy and Favian had emerged from the trees, dragging the two men behind them, Elissa was already kneeling beside the Captain.

"I thought I told you to stay with the boat," said Favian crossly.

"I don't know what they did to him," she said to Billy, ignoring Favian. "He's got a hole in his shoulder." She was trying to stanch the blood with the edge of her robe. "It won't stop bleeding!"

Something had to be done to stop the blood. There were still a couple of drops left in the vial, enough perhaps to give him strength until she could close the wound. She rose and made her way to the still body of Doc. His breathing was light but regular. She felt around his neck for the vial, then searched through his pockets. Nothing.

Billy flung himself beside the Captain, weeping. "Oh, Cappy! Yer dead. Mum'll likely take a cleaver to me."

The Captain's eyelids fluttered. "No such

luck," he said weakly. "Yer mum'll have to make a stew out of somebody else. Probably me. How's Doc?"

Elissa returned and bent close to the Captain. "He's still out," she said softly. "But when he comes to, he's going to have a terrible headache."

"Then he won't be helping us row," said Favian thoughtfully. "We have to get Doc and the Captain to Gravesport."

"What should we do with those two?" asked Elissa, pointing at the motionless bodies of the two hooded men. Even unconscious, they somehow managed to look dangerous.

Favian thought for a moment. "Tie them up for now," he said. "Billy?"

Billy looked relieved to be given a task. "I'll go get some rope," he said, scampering off toward the dinghy.

Elissa took off her robe and wrapped it around the Captain. It was important to keep him warm. "I don't think we'll all fit in the dinghy," she said.

"I know," said Favian. He looked down at the two hooded men and then gazed out toward the water. "Their boat should be around here somewhere." He placed the lantern, which somehow was still lit, beside Elissa and handed her a heavy stick. "I'm going to look for it. If these two wake up, bash them over the head, like so." Favian demonstrated. His black eyes looked down into Elissa's face. "Do you think you can do that?"

"Of course," she replied. In her whole life, Elissa had never struck anybody, person or animal, but in this case she was more than willing to learn. The two men who lay before her were nothing but cold-blooded killers. She hefted the stick. "I'll do just fine."

Once Favian had left, Elissa leaned over the two hooded men, wondering what manner of weapon had injured the Captain. She'd seen a flash, and there had been a loud noise, like a crack of thunder. Then the Captain had fallen to the ground. Could they have burned him somehow? She leaned a bit closer and sniffed; a faint odor of smoke clung to their robes. But the hole in the Captain's shoulder had not looked like a burn. Whatever they had struck him with was like nothing she had seen before. It was fast, invisible, and deadly. In a battle, there would be no defense against it.

"Where's the Count?"

Elissa jumped up, swinging her stick. "Oh, it's you, Billy!" she cried.

Billy caught the end of her stick neatly in one hand. "Sorry, miss," he said. "I brought some rope for these two." He waved a coiled length of rope toward the two robed figures. Elissa released her stick gratefully.

"Favian went to look for the other boat—the one they came in," she said as she stepped aside. While Billy unwound the rope, she picked up the lantern and made her way back to the Captain and Doc.

"How is Cappy?" asked Billy as he tied each man up, joining their hands to their feet behind their backs.

The Captain's normally ruddy face was very pale. She leaned over him; the wound was still bleeding. Elissa patted the big man gently. Then she moved over to where Doc lay, stretched on the ground.

"Doc," she called. "Can you hear me? Wake up, Doc." Elissa put her hand on Doc's shoulder, shaking it very slightly. "Where's the vial?"

Doc's eyelids fluttered, but he didn't answer.

Elissa peered at the murky river. Favian was

taking too long. Perhaps there was no boat. The two men might have come through the swamp on foot. Elissa looked back into the dense undergrowth. No, that would have been impossible. This close to the river, the jungle was nearly impenetrable. No one could make it through on foot, least of all with a heavy load to carry. Elissa thought of the sacks piled on the riverbank and shivered. She suspected that they were full of something terrible, something having to do with that weapon. The splash of oars interrupted her train of thought.

Favian hopped out of a skiff and made his way to Elissa. "There was only one boat, and it's certainly not large enough for all those sacks, so they must be expecting others," he said.

Billy and Favian surveyed the two small vessels. Neither one could take more than three passengers.

"The *Swamp Maiden* must be close by," said Elissa.

Billy nodded. "It'll be at the landing. It's not too far. And likely their dinghy will be hidden somewhere."

"I'm afraid we don't have the time to look," said

Favian. He thought for a moment and came to a decision. "Billy, you take Doc and the Captain. Elissa and I will go ahead of you. If we see anyone, I'll take care of them." In his hand he was holding a slender black cylinder about a foot in length, one end of which was attached to a wooden handle. The other end was open. It smelled of smoke. Elissa shuddered.

"Let's go," said Favian.

"What about those two?" asked Elissa.

Favian looked at the two hooded figures. "I'd like to question them, but there's no room in either boat," he said. "And considering that it's nearly nightfall, it is likely their companions will be coming along shortly. So we'd best leave them as they are."

After Doc and the Captain were loaded into the skiff, Elissa and Favian boarded the dinghy.

"I'll row," said Elissa. "That way your hands will be free, just in case you have to . . ." She let the sentence trail off. The thought of Favian actually using that black cylinder filled her with dread.

As they pulled into the still water, Elissa wondered if they should have done something with Cappy's cargo—hidden it, perhaps. "Maybe we should have looked inside those sacks," she said.

"They were most likely full of these," said Favian, looking down at the cylinder that lay in his lap. Elissa was relieved to see that it was pointed away from her. "Or something related to them."

"Then we should have shoved them all into the river," she said vehemently.

Favian shook his head dismissively. "There wasn't enough time to do a proper job of it. Whoever those two were waiting for would have simply hauled the sacks back out and dried them off. You see, this is made of metal." Favian was peering into the open end of the cylinder.

"Don't do that!" cried Elissa.

Favian turned the cylinder around to scrutinize the other end. "Don't worry," he said. "It's a fairly simple mechanism. It won't work unless I press something along here. Probably this little lever."

"It is a fearsome thing," said Elissa. "I wish you would put it away."

"Then it wouldn't do us much good, would it?" Favian said mildly. He looked at Elissa as she rowed with a firm and steady stroke. "You row quite well," he observed.

"I grew up by a river," she replied. Unbidden, the image of the little eddy where the wood ducks liked to swim rose to her mind—the gentle grassy banks, the smell of Nana's herbs . . .

"Why aren't you afraid of me?" Favian was looking at her curiously.

Elissa looked surprised. "Why should I be?"

"Well, in case you haven't noticed, I am a noble," Favian pointed out. "And you are . . ." Favian raised his eyebrows. "Who exactly are you?"

Elissa kept rowing. She wasn't sure she wanted to answer Favian's question. In all honesty, she wasn't sure she could. So much had happened over the past few months. Was she the same person who had spent most of her life as a poor midwife's apprentice in High Crossing? The one who had climbed barefoot through steep mountain pastures to gather wildflowers and whose sole companion had been a donkey? Or was she Lord Falk's only child, future queen of Castlemar? Somehow, while they were floating down the river on the *Swamp Maiden*, none of that had seemed to matter.

"I'm Elissa," she said simply. That was as close as she could get to the truth, although Favian did not look satisfied with her answer. She knew he wanted a convenient label in order to identify her and put her neatly into a box—peasant, commoner, noble. And now, with her increasingly confusing Gift—well, she could hardly explain *that* to herself, let alone anyone else.

Billy had pulled his boat alongside theirs. Doc was slumped in the bow, rubbing the back of his head.

"How are you, Doc?" called Elissa.

"Ho there, lass," he replied faintly. "A wee bit of a dent, but otherwise none the worse for wear. It's Cappy here I'm worried about." The Captain was propped up in the stern, awake but not looking good.

"I'm sorry, Doc," Elissa said helplessly. "I couldn't stop the bleeding."

"No need to apologize," said Doc. "I don't imagine any of us could."

"Do you have the vial?" asked Elissa.

Doc shook his head slowly. "I left it aboard the *Maiden*," he said. "Didn't want to risk losing it. But there is a healer just around the bend.

Bella will know what to do. If need be, Billy can fetch the vial from the *Maiden*. Then he'll take you to Lily's."

"We should stay with you," said Favian. "For protection."

"No," replied Doc. "It's best you go on with Billy. I can take Cappy into Gravesport when he's fixed up. We're almost there anyway."

It was true. The river had widened considerably, and against its banks were signs of habitation— small docks, ramps, buoys to mark sunken logs. Billy pulled his boat ahead of theirs. Behind them the moon had begun to rise, its pale light shimmering on the water like pools of milk. Within a matter of moments, Billy was pulling his boat to the side of a large, flat rock that jutted out into the water. Elissa's boat drifted alongside Billy's.

"Billy and I will take the Captain up to the house," said Doc. "You two haul the dinghy out of the water and put it behind the rushes, so it'll be hidden. Billy will take you to Gravesport in the skiff." Gently, Billy and Doc eased the Captain out of the skiff and, making a sling with their arms, carried him up a grassy embankment.

The dinghy was so light, Elissa and Favian had no difficulty pulling it out of the water. Once on land, they tipped it over behind the bulrushes that lined the river's edge. Then they pushed the skiff under the overhanging branches of a willow, just to be on the safe side. As it happened, no sooner had they shoved it behind the thick fronds than they heard the sound of voices. Quickly, Favian and Elissa ducked down behind the stand of rushes. Within moments, a cumbersome flat-bottomed barge appeared, poled by four men. It was coming from downriver, from Gravesport.

Favian kept his eyes fixed on the barge as it passed, one hand resting firmly on the hilt of his sword. The other hand held the black cylinder. Although the barge passed within a few yards of their hiding place, Elissa could not make out the faces of the polers. They were all hooded. Elissa held her breath. Only when the barge had completely passed from view did she stir.

"They are moving slowly," said Favian. "We should be safely landed in Gravesport by the time they discover their two companions, load up, and return." He turned toward the embankment. "That is, if Billy hasn't gotten lost on his way back to us."

"I haven't, Count," said Billy matter-of-factly. He emerged suddenly through the dark trees, like a spirit materializing.

"A group of men just passed," said Elissa.

"Yes, I saw them," said Billy. "That's why I waited." He gestured vaguely behind him, toward the darkness. "We'd best stay here the night. Once they find the other two, they'll be looking for us."

"He's right," said Elissa. She had no desire to be chased downriver by a bunch of angry men armed with those firesticks. Elissa and Favian followed Billy up the hill to a tiny cottage set back among the trees. It was situated so that it could not be seen at all from the river.

They passed through a low doorway into a dimly lit room, Billy leading. "I've brought them back," he announced.

"Good work," said Doc. He rose from his position by the hearth, wiping his hands absently on his breeches. Next to him a small woman rose as well. Elissa was surprised to see that she was young and rosy-cheeked.

"Welcome," she said quietly, holding out her hands. "I am Bella. My home is small, but there are mats and blankets enough. And the hearth will keep you warm."

She gestured toward the fire in the grate, beside which a pile of blankets was heaped. The blankets stirred slightly, and Elissa realized that the Captain was lying under them. Bella noticed the direction of her gaze.

"The bleeding has stopped. I've given him a tea to help him sleep while I prepare a poultice," said Bella. "Perhaps you'd like some tea as well?" The woman looked at her so kindly that Elissa agreed without hesitation. Soon she was holding a mug in her hand while Bella fetched rush mats and blankets for them. Doc laid his mat close to the Captain, while Billy and Favian chose positions close to the door. Bella arranged a pallet for Elissa at the center of the room and then bid them all good night before retiring to her little workroom.

Elissa lay on her pallet, gazing at the fire,

while Billy and Favian conferred in low whispers, arranging guard shifts in case they were set upon in the night. Elissa tried to piece together the events of the evening—the men on the barge, the firestick, the Captain falling, the sacks filled with death—but before long she found her eyelids drooping. The last thing she heard was Doc whispering—either to himself or to the Captain, she couldn't tell which—"It's not just the swamp, Cappy. The whole world is changing."

∽ 12 ∽

The Abyss

That night Elissa dreamt she was walking through the jungle. It was dark, but high above her she could see trees leaning in toward one another, their branches touching overhead like arching fingers. They were making a terrible moaning sound, like weeping. Shadow was playing with her feet, pouncing on them. "I can't walk if you do that," she said. She had to go somewhere. It was urgent. But Shadow wouldn't stop playing. Then he started to bite her ankles. "Stop that," she said. "Or I'll tell your mother!" She tried to swat him away, but he kept growling and biting her. "Shadow!" she cried. "Shadow!" She kicked frantically.

"Ouch!" Elissa had stubbed her toe. She found herself standing in the open doorway barefoot, the moonlight filtering through the dark trees. *I must still be dreaming,* she thought. But her toe hurt, so this couldn't be a dream. Then she heard the cry that had roused her.

"Shadow."

It was Night.

Elissa looked back into the room at her sleeping companions. To the right of the door, Favian was sleeping with an arm flung over his face, a lock of dark hair damply plastered to his cheek. On the other side, Billy lay on his back, arms and legs carelessly outspread, lightly snoring. *So much for keeping watch,* she thought.

"Shadow!" The call came again. It was a desperate sound—the cry of a mother who had lost her child.

Automatically, Elissa started walking across the clearing, searching for the cry. It didn't even occur to her to put on her boots or to throw a cloak over her linen shift. The cry seemed to be coming from the river. Then she heard another sound, like the distant crack of thunder. Elissa's breath caught in her throat. She walked faster, toward the river. But once she was standing by the black water, Night's call seemed to come from behind her. She left the river and started walking toward the trees. Once again she heard Night's desperate cry and another sharp report, louder than before. She entered the dark jungle. But now the cry was faint, and somehow diffused. She turned first one way, then another. Night's call seemed to be coming from everywhere.

I'll never find them, she thought. *The trees are creating echoes.* She retraced her steps to the clearing.

Then she heard a howl of intense pain. It stopped her heart. Elissa ran back into the trees, but the jungle was too dense for her to tell where the cry was coming from.

If only I could fly! thought Elissa, pushing through the dark undergrowth. There was a rustling, a deep groaning, and then her path was blocked by two thick branches. Elissa grasped them with both hands. But before she could push them aside, the branches scooped her up with a smooth sweeping motion and catapulted her into the air.

Elissa soared above the jungle. *Now I know I'm dreaming,* she thought. The full moon shone brightly in the sky, illuminating the tops of the trees. Stars twinkled. A light breeze caught the fabric of her shift and, like wings, it fluttered against her ribs. It was a breathless moment in which Elissa felt no fear, only the buoyant ease of flight. So this was how it felt to be a bird! Then she started to drop.

"Catch me!" she called. Leafy branches reached up for her, wrapping around her arms and legs, cradling her gently until her feet touched the ground. Then they released her, springing up and away, leaving Elissa standing in a dense thicket beside the river. She heard Night's cry again, this time from somewhere very close.

She must be near the river, Elissa thought, struggling with the hanging vines that dripped from every branch. The underbrush was so dense, she was forced back away from the riverbank. She tripped over a root. *I'll never get there,* she thought.

Elissa stopped, remembering the direction from which the cry had come. "Clear the way," she said, holding out her arms. Immediately, the vines receded and the bracken drew aside. A clear path opened ahead of her. Elissa ran lightly between the trees. Tangled roots slithered away from her like snakes returning to their lairs, leaving smooth ground beneath her feet. Within moments she had emerged into a small moonlit patch of jungle. A dark pool lay at its center. Elissa approached cautiously. "Night?" she called.

A shadow drew up from the ground and a pair of glowing yellow eyes met hers.

"He does not answer," said Night.

Elissa put her hand on Night's back and leaned over the cat's powerful shoulder, suddenly afraid of what she might see.

On the ground, Shadow's dark, furry body lay still in the moonlight. Night nosed her cub gently, but there was no answering movement. There was not even the gentle rise and fall of breathing. Elissa bent down and touched his body. A sharp metallic odor drifted up to her nostrils as she drew her hand back. Shadow's fur was wet, sticky with blood.

Elissa made a strangled little sound, a wordless cry of grief. The moonlit trees blurred with her tears. Then the world seemed to lurch beneath her feet, but it was only a sob that shook her from her head to her toes. Elissa clutched the fur on Night's back to steady herself. Night leaned against her, eyes closed in quiet despair.

A sound broke the silence. Laughter.

Elissa straightened up and turned toward the sound, like an animal scenting prey. "Come with me," she whispered.

Elissa walked through the jungle on silent, purposeful feet, Night moving fluidly at her side like a dark river. She didn't know where she was going or what she intended to do when she got there, but the sounds of celebration and the sharp reports of the firesticks—for that was surely what they were—drew her on like a magnet. Staring straight ahead, like a sleepwalker, she scarcely noticed the trees that drew back from her on either side of her path. The image of Shadow's still body wholly occupied her mind. She stopped only when something squelched beneath her feet. It was a small puddle of blood.

Elissa looked around and for the first time took note of her surroundings. A small trail of feathers was scattered alongside the path, and there was evidence of the recent passing of people.

The bracken had been trampled underfoot, and branches carelessly broken.

There was another crack, and then shouting. Night stiffened, and the fur along her spine rose. Elissa felt a chill creep up her cheeks and along her scalp.

All at once, the trees gave way to a clearing. A bright bonfire danced at its center, dazzling Elissa's eyes. She made out dark forms cavorting around the fire, waving black cylinders in the air, accompanied by the sound of raucous laughter. Elissa laid a hand on Night's neck to steady herself while her eyes adjusted.

"Ho!" A voice shouted over the laughter. "Shut up! We've got visitors."

There was a silence. One of the men advanced.

"It's just a girl!" The man stood in front of the campfire, holding a slender cylinder in his hand—a firestick. He had the confident swagger of a leader and the obvious intent to use the weapon. Elissa ignored him. She was looking past the man at his companions, who either lay sprawled on the ground, empty bottles by their sides, or stood in various postures of surprise. Elissa finally focused on the dark carcasses scattered around a tree at the other end of the clearing. One of them seemed to be moving. A small, furry body was attached to the tree by a short rope. It struggled against the rope, scratching ineffectually at the tree bark with its fingers.

"Fools!" cried the monkey.

"Will somebody just shoot that thing?" said the leader. "I'm tired of hearing it squawk."

"Don't be stupid," said one of the men. "The others were just trash, but that one's worth good money in Gravesport."

"Well, if you won't shut it up, I will." The leader raised his firestick, and a second later a loud crack split the night. An acrid smell filled the air. Resting his smoking weapon on his shoulder, the man turned—to face a pair of blazing emerald eyes.

"Night—" said Elissa, lifting her hand from the *yagua*'s neck.

Before the man could fire his weapon again— indeed, before he could take a breath or even register the fact that the dark shadow beside the white-clad young girl had moved—he found himself flat on his back, two hundred pounds of sinew crushing his chest. His eyes rolled in his head like marbles.

"Now?" asked Night. The *yagua* waited for Elissa's command, although she never lifted her great yellow eyes from the man's terrified face.

The other men were beginning to realize something had happened. From around the fire, the upright ones advanced, while others rose from the ground, reaching for their deadly fire-sticks.

"Not yet," said Elissa. The sharp-faced man who lay paralyzed just inches below Night's dripping fangs looked familiar. He was the one who had shot the Captain. She shifted her eyes from him to the men who were now advancing, focusing their sight on the slender white form gleaming in the firelight. They were moving very slowly, their heads and limbs heavy with drink. For a moment, time seemed to stand still. Elissa looked at the vines draped innocently along the tree limbs. Then something surged through her. It flowed straight up her spine like a wave and expanded through her chest, filling her with a deep sense of power. A simple picture formed in her mind—vines surrounding men. There was no need for clumsy words. No need for thoughts or commands. It was effortless.

The men, in their woozy state, could not understand what was happening to them. Some had the presence of mind to hold on to their firesticks. A few even had a chance to discharge them. But not having a clear view of their leader, who was lying motionless at Elissa's feet, or an understanding of what was happening, they simply fired their weapons uselessly into the trees. In any event, the vines—which had encircled them in a living net, binding their arms and legs and immobilizing their heads and hands—soon encased their firesticks as well. Some of the more alert among them tried to run. But within seconds the solid ground, which had always lain dormant beneath their feet, had become a seething mass of tendrils that now rose up and ensnared them. Soon they were unrecognizable as men. The clearing merely looked as if it had sprouted new trees.

And in that space there was not a sound.

Elissa looked about her, her eyes not seeming to register that there were men standing before her grasped within the tight fist of the jungle. Her scalp twitched. It was not the first time she had felt grief. Nor was it the first time she had felt anger. But it was the first time she had experienced rage. The men, the fire, the poor monkey, Night, Shadow—all of it faded into a red haze. Elissa knew with absolute certainty that she could end their lives right here, right now—their pointless destruction, their arrogance, their cruelty. Night waited to do her bidding, as did the entire jungle. She could simply give the command—anytime. *Now.*

Before Elissa could utter the command, a sharp crack disturbed the silence of the waiting jungle. She whirled around, but it was not the thunder of a firestick—just a twig snapping underfoot, echoing in the stillness. Slowly, a figure emerged from the darkness.

"This one is still alive," said Doc. He was barefoot and moved carefully over the exposed roots and writhing vines. There was something furry in his arms.

Elissa felt as if she were teetering at the brink of a bottomless chasm, about to fall. The gaping pit yawned, ready to swallow her. She knew that once she started falling—once she gave the order to kill—she'd fall forever. Doc held out his arms.

Elissa exhaled, and the red haze began to lift. It seemed that she had not breathed in a very long time. The heavy jungle air flowed into her rage-frozen lungs, expanding and contracting them—sweet with life. Night turned her head toward Doc and growled deep in her throat.

"No, Night," said Elissa. "He is a friend." She began to walk toward Doc, and with each step she felt herself backing away from the abyss. Keeping his eyes fixed on Night, who had silently drifted to Elissa's side, Doc cautiously handed Shadow to Elissa.

"How?" she asked, cradling Shadow. He was warm and breathing.

"After you fell asleep, I went back to the *Maiden* to fetch the vial for Cappy," said Doc, drawing the silver vial from his shirt. "But Bella said he was going to pull through just fine—Cappy's a tough old goat—so I decided not to use it quite yet. When I heard all the noise, I came after you. There was only a drop left. And this creature is so little, I guess it was enough."

Elissa knelt down and gently laid Shadow on

the ground before Night's great paws. Night sniffed at her son and then, closing her eyes, began to stroke him from head to tail with her long rough tongue.

Shadow murmured weakly, "Don't do that, Mama," but he held still. A moment later, Night caught him up by the nape of his neck and disappeared into the jungle.

Once the cats were gone, the leader, who until that point had not dared move a muscle, got up and ran off on wobbly legs, leaving his men to fend for themselves.

Elissa gave him a brief, unconcerned glance and turned back to the spot where the cats had disappeared.

"Shadow will be all right," she murmured, trying to reassure herself.

"Aye," said Doc softly. "But will you?"

Elissa took a deep, shuddering breath. Her charged body went limp, and she was suddenly on the verge of tears. "Oh, Doc!" she cried, waving her arms incoherently at the jungle, the carcasses, the men encased in vines. "Look at what they did! And for *what*? *Why did they do this?*"

"I can't tell you, lass," said Doc, his eyes gentle

in his weathered face. He shook his head slowly and took Elissa by the hand. "I can't explain what is in men's hearts. And I can't explain what I just saw. I can only watch and wait for the truth."

Elissa held on to Doc's hand. He was shorter than she was, but she felt as if she were being lifted up. "The truth," she said slowly, "is that animals don't take vengeance. It is not in their nature. And I . . . I was . . ." Elissa paused, unable to continue. "Perhaps I am just as bad as *they* are."

Doc smiled. "No, lass. You're just human." He tilted his head back, giving Elissa a long look. "Well, maybe not."

Elissa stood in silence, her thoughts traveling to a dark land she had never visited.

"Fools!"

Elissa turned to see a small, furry body flinging itself furiously against the tree. "You're alive!" she cried.

"Well, of course I'm alive!" shrieked the monkey. "Stop dawdling over there and do something useful!"

Elissa pulled her hand free from Doc's. They made their way around the fire to the tree where the monkey was tied. While Elissa undid the knot, Doc picked up the firesticks that lay scattered on the ground, tucking them into his shirt, his belt, his breeches. As soon as she was released, the monkey ran straight up the tree trunk and vanished into the leaves of the canopy.

"You're welcome," murmured Elissa.

Laden with weapons, Doc walked up to one of the men, who was holding a firestick tight in his vine-wrapped hand. "I can't get at this one," he said. He looked around at the other men in similar positions. "Or those."

"All right," said Elissa. She formed a mental picture of the vines loosening from the men's hands, and as the vines unraveled, the remaining weapons plopped to the ground. Through all of this, none of the men uttered a sound. Indeed, most of them hardly dared to breathe.

"What should we do with these?" Doc asked, pointing at the firesticks.

Elissa glanced at the fire. "I don't think they'll burn," she said.

"And who knows what would happen if fire met fire," observed Doc.

Elissa looked up pensively into the trees. "I

wouldn't want them to fall into other hands." She returned to an earlier thought. "We'll throw them in the river," she said.

Together, Doc and Elissa gathered up the rest of the weapons and, making their way to the riverbank, threw them into the center of the current.

"No one will dive for them here," said Doc with satisfaction. "There are water creatures in these parts that have a taste for human flesh."

Yes, thought Elissa, *Serena will guard them for me.* When the last firestick had been thrown into the swirling depths of the river, Doc and Elissa returned to the clearing. There Doc turned bright, expectant eyes on Elissa.

Elissa looked at the men in their vine cages. If she left them that way, eventually they would die of hunger. Or perhaps their leader would return and cut them loose. Or perhaps the jungle beasts would discover that here was easy prey. Elissa shook her head, defeated by her own conscience. She pictured the vines returning to the jungle. Startled, Doc took a step backward as the vines slithered over the ground.

"Don't worry," said Elissa. "They won't hurt you."

Doc blew a little puff of air from between his lips. "That's reassuring," he said. But he watched until at last the vines rested, seemingly inert, upon the branches of the trees.

The men, who now had control over their legs, wasted not a moment but ran as quickly as they could into the jungle, which, for all its many dangers, did not compare to the terror produced by a single green-eyed girl.

Elissa briefly assessed the deserted clearing, as if fixing it in her mind, and then said simply, "Let's go." She turned and took a step toward the shelter of the trees.

"Wait—" said Doc. "I have to know." His eyes were wide, imploring. "Are you a goddess?"

Elissa sucked in her breath, feeling the depths of the abyss she had just been saved from. Her Gift was something she could never explain— not to Maya, or to Doc, or even to herself. It had simply felt natural—and safe. Up until now, she had never thought her Gift could be used to do harm. Now Elissa was unsure of her place in the world. It had changed—no, it was *she* who had changed. She had nearly gone against Nature, and, in so doing, she had come close to destroying more than a few men with firesticks ever could. Elissa looked into Doc's eyes, coming to a decision.

"I don't really know what I am anymore," she said, her eyes dark. "But I do know I must never do *that* again."

The Mermaid Inn

To her immense relief, given the disturbing events of the evening, Elissa fell asleep easily and quickly after a brief "Sleep well" and a pat on the head from Doc. There was something comforting about telling Doc that she would not use her powers again. She felt released from an unwanted burden. In a way, she felt restored to herself, which told her that she had not been feeling herself for a while. *This kind of power was not meant for mere mortals,* she thought as she drifted into oblivion. Her mood must have influenced her dreams, because she found herself back in High Crossing, sitting by Nana's hearth.

There were four pots in the fire. "Mind the pots," said Nana. Elissa leaned forward to stir them, but there was no stirring spoon. Nor was there any liquid in them to stir, save for one, which contained only clear water. The other three pots held things that somehow, within the context of the dream, made perfect sense to Elissa—dirt, fire, and a small white flower. "Go fetch me the other pot," said Nana. Elissa looked around but did not see another pot. "I'll get it for you," said Elissa, rising. When she began to move, she woke up.

Even after Elissa realized where she was, Nana's instructions lingered in her mind. She stretched luxuriously on her pallet, momentarily freed from the complexities of her life, knowing that all she had to do was find a clay pot.

"You're awake," said Doc. He was perched on a little three-legged stool by her pallet.

"Oh!" said Elissa. "Have I slept late?"

"A bit," said Doc, handing her a bowl of hot gruel. "But you needed it."

As she took the bowl between her hands, she asked where the others had gone.

"Billy and the Count are readying the skiff to take you to Gravesport," said Doc.

"Will you come, too?" asked Elissa. She felt a pang of sorrow at the thought of leaving Doc.

There was something comforting about the old man. Paradoxically, the fact that he had witnessed the worst in her settled her mind. For the first time since she had lost Maya, she felt as if she had someone to turn to.

Doc shook his head. "No, I'll be staying here with Cappy just a little while longer. We'll meet you at Billy's mother's house." His weathered face crinkled in a smile. "Don't worry, you'll be safe."

Elissa wasn't really worried about her own safety in Gravesport. If anything, Gravesport might be a little less safe with *her* in it! Her Gift had increased alarmingly, to the point where she no longer understood it. What if she lost her temper again and actually killed somebody—just with a thought?

"Is it too hot?" asked Doc. "You haven't eaten a bite."

Elissa realized that she had completely forgotten about the bowl of gruel resting in her lap.

"I'm not really hungry," Elissa said. She took a deep breath. "I'm a little worried about what happened last night."

Doc patted her hand. "I'm afraid those

weapons are here to stay," he said. "No matter how many we throw into the river."

Elissa shook her head. "No, I mean about what I did. What if I do something truly awful someday?"

Doc pursed his lips thoughtfully. "You won't," he said. "Your heart is too kind."

"But what if it's not on purpose?"

"You'll control yourself," said Doc simply.

Elissa squeezed her eyes shut. She remembered the surge of power that had flowed through her. *I'll simply have to learn to master it,* she thought. When she opened her eyes, Doc was gone and the sun was shining innocently and uneventfully, as it always did. *Today,* she said to herself, *is going to be just a plain old normal day.*

After a brief farewell to the Captain, who was looking pale but breathing deeply and evenly, Elissa set off for Gravesport. She sat in the stern of the skiff while Favian took the bow, holding a short pole in his hands to move aside any branches or floating debris that might impede their progress. Billy sat at the oars, pulling cheerfully and humming to himself. Much to everyone's relief, they did not get lost. By late afternoon, the river had widened considerably and they could smell the sea.

"You see!" said Billy, triumphant. "I know these parts like the palm of my hand."

"There's only one waterway," said Favian. "And it's as wide as a wheat field. Unless you picked up the boat and walked it to Gravesport, there's no way we *could* have gotten lost!"

Billy took Favian's retort with good humor. "Well," he said with a wink, "I got us here, didn't I?"

Billy landed the skiff just before sunset, or so Elissa thought. The sky turned a dark gray as they neared Gravesport, and it was impossible to see the sun. Although there were a number of boats tied to the rusty rings that lined the sides of the docks, there was not a soul in sight. Elissa asked why no one from the Dock Authority was waiting to meet them.

"This section of the docks is only used by locals," explained Billy. "It's not big enough for the larger cargo boats. So the authorities don't bother coming around." He tied the line to a metal ring. "Me mum's place isn't far."

They disembarked and made their way rapidly past the deserted wharves. Squat, ugly warehouses lined the docks, their hollow windows looking ominous in the waning light. The wharves were very dirty. Mounds of garbage lay in haphazard heaps against the buildings. They most likely had been blown there by the wind, as the wharves looked untouched by human hands—or brooms. Elissa saw four little paws sticking out stiffly from one of the mounds. She shuddered. Her first impression of the port was not reassuring in the least. She hoped that when they entered the residential district, she would find the place more cheerful. However, as they made their way deeper into the city, Elissa's unease only increased.

Every street they walked along was cold, silent, and dreary beyond description. After the continuous clamor of the riverside, the profound silence of the city shocked her. That low hum—the sound of the jungle with its teeming life—was completely absent, as was animal talk of any kind. Could it be that in Gravesport there was not a single live animal? Or maybe in this cold place the pigeons dared not coo, the rats feared to squeak. Even weeds seemed afraid to grow here. There was not a single tree or plant of any kind to be seen. The roads were paved entirely with flat gray stones that continued up the straight walls of the buildings to either side. To Elissa, it looked as though the whole city had been constructed of the same hard, unyielding rock. As night fell, the fog rolled in from the sea, cloaking the buildings in a damp shroud. The overall effect was dismal. To top it off, the place stank. The combined odor of dead fish, rotting garbage, and excrement was unbearable. As they hurried along, Elissa tried to filter the stench by breathing through the cloth of her robe. While holding her wide sleeve against her nose, she nearly tripped into a ditch.

Favian caught Elissa by her elbow. "Open sewers. Very unsanitary," he said. Then he quickly dropped his hand.

Elissa stopped for a moment. She had felt the heat of his palm straight through her robe. She wondered if he still had a touch of fever.

"Come along," cried Billy. He flitted in front

of them, his shirt a white smear against the gray stones. For a brief moment, Elissa wondered if he might be related to a gull.

They continued on through the dark, deserted streets. Once they passed another hurrying figure. Greetings were not exchanged.

"Most decent folks are in by now," explained Billy.

Elissa could understand why. The empty streets and looming buildings had an air of menace about them. The three of them wandered interminably, or at least it seemed so to Elissa. Every building looked the same to her—every street corner, every alleyway and passage—unvarying in its dull, lifeless gray. Even the darkening sky, or what she could see of it through the mist, was gray. Elissa wondered how anyone could live here. She felt her spirits sinking, her steps slowing. The ground felt hard beneath her feet—ungiving, lifeless. Even if she had wanted to use her powers here, she couldn't. The cold gray stone would stop them. And soon she would stop walking, stop caring . . .

"We're almost there!" Billy's shout broke

Elissa free of her doldrums. She lifted her head and quickened her pace. In just a few moments they would pass through a doorway, and on the other side they would find light, warmth, and food. They rounded a corner and stopped. Billy lifted his cap and scratched his head.

"Oh no," groaned Elissa. "Not again."

"It was right here, I swear it," cried Billy. "Now, where can Mum have got to?" He walked up and down the narrow street, examining stones, doorways, shuttered windows. "She must have moved," he concluded. "But where to?"

"Can we ask?" Elissa was sure that if they just rapped on a door, someone would surely tell them where Billy's mother lived. She raised her hand in a loose fist.

"Don't do that," warned Billy. "It's too late for knocking."

Favian had not said a word for quite some time, but at the alarm in Billy's voice, he tightened his grip on his sword. "We'll find an inn for the night," he said. "There should be several close to the passenger-ship docks." He turned and gestured for them to follow. To Elissa's surprise, he seemed to know exactly where to go. "Long experience as a hunter," he added. "I make it a habit to know where I am."

Elissa followed his sure strides with relief. Wherever they were headed, she felt more confident with Favian in the lead.

Soon they came to a street hung with signs. She stood close to one and peered up at it. The sign was nothing more than a cracked oar, on which were painted a bowl, a mug, and a copper.

"If you pay a penny, you get a penny's worth of hospitality," said Favian. "Let's go on." He marched upon the damp cobbles, striking them defiantly with his bootheels. "The quality of these establishments will improve as we approach the far end of the docks. That's where the larger ships berth."

Billy gazed at Favian in admiration. "Have ye been here b'fore, sir?" he inquired politely. Favian, preoccupied with his thoughts or memories, did not answer. Billy didn't seem to mind. At this point, nothing Favian could say or not say would have diminished Billy's esteem for him.

Favian was soon proven right, for after they'd passed half a dozen similar inns, the quality of the signs began to improve, as did their artistry. At a sign depicting a beautiful maiden, he halted. "This will do," pronounced Favian. Billy and Elissa made to enter, but he waved them back. "Let me go in first," he said.

The two of them waited under the sign. It was a skillfully painted portrait. The maiden sat upon a greenish rock surrounded by waves, her long brown tresses blowing in the breeze. Both of her slim arms were raised to hold her hair away from her lovely face. Elissa thought it odd that the artist had not painted her legs. The lower half of the maiden's body seemed to melt into the sea. The face, however, was where the artist had shown his true skill. The eyes were so lifelike, they seemed to follow Elissa wherever she stood. As Elissa looked up at the sign, the maiden gazed down upon Elissa, her eyes soft and deep. They were Maya's eyes.

The door suddenly opened wide, releasing a flood of light onto the street. "Come in!" boomed a deep voice. "Welcome to the Mermaid Inn!"

The Mermaid Inn proved to be a cheery place, well lit by a roaring fire and smelling cleanly of fresh sawdust. Surprisingly, they appeared to be the only guests. No sooner had the proprietor seated them at a table by the fire than a rosy-cheeked serving maid set three steaming bowls of thick potato soup and a plate of fried smelts before them. A moment later, the bread boy appeared with loaves of warm, fragrant bread and a jug of ale.

"How will we pay for this?" whispered Elissa. She knew that between the three of them, they possessed not one penny.

"Don't worry about that," said Favian. "Just eat."

Needing no further encouragement, Elissa and Billy tucked into their dinners with enthusiasm. Favian, however, ate cautiously. He had positioned himself with his back to the fire, facing the door.

"Is everything to your satisfaction, Count?" The host of the establishment had sidled up to the table. He smiled broadly, showing off a full set of yellowing teeth. His brow was beaded with sweat, which he mopped with the hem of his white apron.

Favian nodded curtly.

"Contessa?" the host inquired of Elissa. He

looked at her expectantly, rubbing his hands together nervously in front of his ample belly.

Elissa felt Favian's foot nudge hers, gently but
firmly, under the table. She nodded, mimicking
Favian's remote, self-contained expression. She
was beginning to understand their situation.
"Quite," she murmured.

"We will be retiring soon," said Favian. "Best
to treat us just like all your other guests," he
added in a low voice.

The proprietor pulled on his earlobe and
winked knowingly. "Yes, yes, of course," he said.
He leaned close and proclaimed, "I will reveal
your true identities to no one!" Then he waddled
off, shouting for the serving girl.

Favian winced. But after their host had disappeared, he glanced at Elissa and gave her a rare,
brief smile. She had played her part to perfection.

"Girl! More ale!"

Apparently there was one other guest. A
swarthy man, seated at the far end of the room,
clapped his mug down on the table. The flickering light of the fire did not illuminate that end of
the room very well, but what Favian could see of

the man was unpleasant. Like a mismatched puzzle, the two sides of his face did not fit together. A blade had gouged his left eye from its socket. The scar that crossed the empty pit traversed the length of the man's cheek to his stubbled jaw, which folded in at that point, narrowing the entire side of his face. The other, intact, side of his face was lean, dark, predatory. The man kept a sullen eye on the pretty serving girl as she refreshed his mug. She could not have been more than a dozen years old.

"That's better," the man rasped. When he lifted his head to speak, Favian saw that the scar traveled downward, crossing his throat. Someone had made a serious effort to kill this man—and the man's general demeanor indicated that he had deserved it and might very well deserve it again sometime soon.

The serving girl removed the empty carafe and looked up, smiling, in their direction. She nodded and indicated with a raised forefinger that their room was ready. Balancing her tray against her hip, she turned to walk toward their table.

The man lifted his mug as if to drink and

then seemed to change his mind. "I know you're deaf, girl, but are you dumb as well?"

The girl stopped in confusion. "Sir?" she inquired.

"When I say, 'That's better,' you say, 'Thank ye kindly, sir!'"

"Thank ye kindly, sir," stammered the girl.

"That's better," grumbled the man.

The girl resumed her course toward their table but had not advanced more than a pace when the man reached out and grabbed her skirt.

"You're dumber than a post! What did I just say?" The man's raspy voice was low, but it had carrying power.

"That's better," repeated the girl. "Oh dear— thank ye kindly, sir."

Once again the man said, "That's better." And once more the girl began to walk away. He grabbed her long braid before she could pass out of reach. It was clear from the expression on his face that he enjoyed this game. The girl stopped short, her face twisted in pain.

"Thank . . . ye . . . kindly . . . sir," she said, trying to free herself.

"That's—"

Unlike Favian, the man at the table had not kept an eye on the other occupants of the room. In midsentence, the one-eyed man found himself suspended, tightly gripped in the arms of a brawny sailor.

"—better." Favian quietly finished the man's statement. He was holding the point of his sword against the man's throat. "Have you been served?" The man made the slightest of nods. Favian removed his sword and, without taking his eyes from the man's face, said, "You can put him down now."

Billy dropped the man gently into his chair and smoothed his rumpled jacket in a solicitous manner. The man sat still, rubbing his throat, his face averted.

"That's better," said Favian with a smile. He looked at the man pointedly and waited. Elissa could not see the man's face from across the room, but even at this distance she could see the red sparks flashing in Favian's eyes.

"Thank ye kindly, sir," said the man, sounding somewhat breathless.

Neither Favian nor Billy replied. They merely turned their backs on him and followed the young serving girl back to their table, where Elissa stood waiting. Ushering Elissa ahead of them out of the common room, they mounted the stairs to the inn's sleeping quarters. And so it was that Favian missed the look the man cast in their direction—sheer loathing mixed with something even more disturbing: satisfaction. When the small group had left, the one-eyed man sipped his ale and contemplated the twists and turns of fate. "All things come to he who waits," he murmured. He spread his lopsided lips in a sharklike grin over what remained of his large pointed teeth.

Elissa did not know what had roused her, but once she was awake, she realized she needed to find the privy. Billy was snoring on the floor beside the door, and Favian was sleeping soundly on the bed across from hers. This was the inn's most elegant room, boasting not one but two real beds. Most of the other rooms were furnished with simple straw mattresses, like the one she had slept on at home. She would have been perfectly happy to sleep on sweet-smelling straw, but Favian would not allow it. Now that the innkeeper thought her a countess, she'd better act like one, he said—as if she knew how. Elissa rose silently and, wrapping her robe tightly around her, tiptoed carefully across the room. If her nose had served her right, she would find the outhouse in the courtyard they had passed on their way up to the sleeping rooms.

She made her way down the narrow passageway, keeping her hands outstretched before her in the dark. It was long past midnight, so all the candles in the wall sconces had been extinguished. She remembered that there was a stairway just a few paces to the left, then another passageway. Elissa thought the courtyard could not be far. As she suspected, it wasn't. She took another three steps and found herself in the open. Then she heard it—a deep, heart-wrenching moan.

Hearing the sound jogged Elissa's memory. This was what had awakened her—this unearthly cry of pain. She heard it again, and the sound filled her heart with sadness. She looked up. The moaning seemed to be emanating from the other side of the courtyard. She made her way through the yard, avoiding the piles of trash that littered the cobblestones. It was not easy going; the courtyard seemed to serve as a rubbish pit for all manner of broken tools and equipment. At one point, Elissa's robe got snagged on a sharp-edged object resembling a scythe. She freed herself from it with some difficulty.

The closer she drew to the source of the keening, the more melancholy she became. Whatever creature was making this sound was in agony. It sounded hopelessly alone, trapped, afraid. Elissa's resolve hardened. Once she had found the creature, she vowed to set it free.

Just ahead of her, Elissa spied the outline of a narrow door frame. It was set beneath a stairway leading to another wing of the inn, perhaps to additional sleeping rooms or to the innkeeper's quarters. From its location, Elissa judged that the room behind it must be quite small—a storeroom of some kind. However, when she drew closer she saw that the door was barred on the outside. Perhaps the room was meant to keep someone or something imprisoned, though a person with free hands and a stick might easily have escaped, as the door hung loosely from its frame. A four-pawed animal, on the other hand, would be trapped. Elissa studied the door and counted herself fortunate. Had the room been securely locked, she would not have been able to enter it so easily. Another deep, terrible moan came from within. Elissa lifted the bar and the door swung back. The hinges were well oiled and made only the barest of creaks, but the sound was enough to make the moaning stop.

Elissa stood just inside the doorway for a moment or two, allowing her eyes to adjust to the dark. The only opening was the door, so the room was pitch-black inside. From what Elissa could see, it was empty, save for a large box that had been pushed deep into the shadows. Silently, she drew closer. Bars extended around the sides of the box and over the top. It was a cage. She put her hand out experimentally. The bars were made of cold, smooth metal. Elissa bent down close to the cage, trying to see through the bars. She heard rapid, shallow breathing.

"Don't be afraid," she whispered. "I won't hurt you." Elissa did not know what kind of creature was trapped inside, but she knew that all animals understood her. No matter what manner of beast was caged within these bars, she could calm it with just a few words.

A frail hand reached out through the bars to touch Elissa's hair. "I am not afraid of you."

Elissa drew back, stunned. The poor creature inside the cage was not a beast, but a person. And from the pitch and timbre of the voice, it was a woman. A patch of white hair gleamed against the bars. Elissa felt a sudden flush of anger. What monster would lock an old woman up in a cage?

"I'll get you out of here," she promised. "Is there a door?"

"Here." The hand guided Elissa around to the front of the cage. "It's locked."

Though the woman's hand was steady, her voice was curiously breathy, insubstantial. Elissa thought she must be very old indeed. She felt along the edge of the door and found the lock. It was heavy, but not very complicated. Elissa thought that she might be able to pick it. She felt inside the pockets of her robe for her fibula and almost laughed. She had known Sohar's gift would come in handy someday.

Elissa's triumph was short-lived, however.

The lock was more complicated than she had thought, and the room was too dark for her to work. She poked around with the fibula as best she could, but it soon became apparent that without light, opening the lock was a lost cause.

"If I only had a candle," she muttered. Then, in the next instant, she heard a sound that made her heart stop. Someone was coming through the door. She leapt up and whirled around, fibula in hand—just a second too late.

"I thought I'd find you here," said a voice. A strong hand grasped Elissa by the wrist, forcing the fibula from her hand. It fell at her feet, clanging uselessly against the stone.

⇜ 14 ⇝

Sounds of Pursuit

"Favian!" gasped Elissa.

Favian picked up the fibula and handed it to Elissa. "Do forgive me," he said. "I could not, in good conscience, allow you to stab my eyes out. You would have felt wretched about it afterward."

"How did you find me?" Elissa was still breathing hard from her shock.

Favian was peering inquisitively into the cage. "As I said, I have long experience as a hunter," he murmured. "I followed your trail. What's inside?"

"Someone has locked an old woman in there. You have to help me get her out!" Elissa held up the fibula, hoping Favian could see it. "I can pick the lock, but I need a light," she explained.

"I happen to have one right here," said Favian.

He held his hands out. Within Favian's cupped palms Elissa could see the glow of a candle. She breathed a sigh of relief. The rest should be easy.

"Let's hurry," suggested Favian. "If someone comes, I won't be able to hold the light and my sword at the same time."

Elissa acknowledged that he had a point. Whoever had locked up the old woman might be returning at any moment. She worked quickly. Within a few minutes, she was gratified to hear the sound of the lock releasing. She carefully lifted up the heavy lock and pulled at the bars. As soon as the cage door swung back, she reached her arm inside.

"You can come out now," she said in a soft voice. She waited a moment. There was only silence. Then, with a slight rustling, the old woman emerged.

She was surprisingly tall and very, very thin. Her downturned face was hidden by a mass of pale hair. *Poor thing*, thought Elissa. *They have starved her.* "Come," she said, beckoning. "We'll take you to a safe place."

In truth, Elissa had no idea how safe their

room might be, given the clientele of this establishment. But anything was better than standing here in this dank, cramped room under the
stairs. The three of them made their way rapidly
through the courtyard in single file. Elissa found
the journey much easier with the help of Favian,
who led the way with his little light. As Elissa
followed behind the old woman, she marveled at
how tall she was. Even in her bare feet, she stood
a full head taller than Favian. There was something odd about her hair. It floated away from her
head in tufts, as though it had no weight. It reminded Elissa of something familiar.

As they passed the spot where Elissa had
snagged her robe, Favian stopped and deliberately removed a shred of dark cloth from the
hook. She caught the barest hint of a smile as he
turned his head away.

Ha! she thought. *Long experience as a hunter,
indeed. I'll bet a blind man could have followed me.*

They hurried back toward the passageway
that led to their room, the old woman and Elissa
following close behind Favian's flickering candle.
When they arrived at the door, however, Favian
stopped short. The candle went out. Elissa was

afraid to say anything, afraid to make a sound. For she, too, had realized that something was amiss. The door was not quite shut. The woman, frightened by their hesitation, dropped into a crouch, protecting her head with her arms. Elissa reached out a hand to steady her.

So soft, thought Elissa as her hand touched the woman's pale hair. *It's exactly like down.* Feeling Elissa's hand, the woman lifted her head, and for the first time Elissa caught a glimpse of her features. She caught her breath in surprise.

There wasn't a line on the woman's face.

Elissa heard the metallic hiss of Favian's sword as he drew it from its sheath. Thinking fast, she pulled the woman away from the door, back into the hallway. There was no point getting in the way of Favian's sword, or of whoever might shortly find himself at the other end of it. Silently Favian counted to three, kicked the door open, and entered, his sword at the ready. There was a sudden stillness. Elissa peered around the corner of the doorway.

Favian had sheathed his sword and somehow lit his candle again, bathing the room in soft light. It was empty, except for Billy lying on the bed, trussed up like a Solstice goose and with a rag tied around his mouth. He must not have been in that position long, for he was still struggling. Quickly, Elissa made her way to him, took the rag from his mouth, and set about releasing him.

"Gaw," he gasped. "I thought it was *him*! That one-eyed man."

Reflexively, Favian's hand twitched toward his sword. With a soft moan, the woman slumped against the side of the bed.

"He's going to come back for you and the miss—with more of his friends." Billy's tone was urgent. "The man's bonkers, kept rattling on about justice. And they had one of those things that put a hole in Cappy. I think they're sailants!"

"Pirates, more like it," said Favian. "Hurry!"

"I can't get these undone," gasped Elissa. She was having a great deal of difficulty freeing Billy from his bonds. The knots that bound Billy were impossible to untangle, even with the woman's help. There were so many of them and not enough time.

"Hand me the candle," she said. "I'll set it down right here. Help me get these knots loose."

Favian was curiously reluctant to give her the light. "You'll get burned," he said. "I'll hold it."

"But they could be back any moment," protested Elissa.

"I can take care of them." There was a stubborn tone in Favian's voice that Elissa recognized. He would tolerate no discussion.

"Not without this . . . ," she said. Before he could protest, Elissa reached around Favian's waist and drew his razor-sharp sword from its sheath. In short order she sliced through the remaining knots. While the woman helped Billy up from the bed, Elissa turned to hand the sword back to Favian. As she held it out to him, the light in Favian's hands caught the gems in the hilt, making them sparkle. But something was different—the large gem was missing! So that was how he had paid for their night in the inn.

"Sheathe it for me," mumbled Favian. "If you would."

It wasn't like Favian to mumble or to ask her for a favor. All at once, Elissa had a hunch. She forced the sword into his hands.

Suddenly the light went out. The woman

yelped as Billy, somewhat stiff from his bondage, crashed awkwardly into her.

"Sorry, marm! Where'd the blasted light go?" Billy cried.

In the darkness, Elissa drew close to Favian, cupping her hand around his ear.

"Can you do that with one hand?" she whispered in a voice as low as the flutter of a moth's wing.

Favian hesitated. He leaned down and murmured, "Yes, but it won't be as bright."

"We'll manage," she whispered.

A small light sprang up. The group clustered close behind Favian, but only Elissa, who had pressed herself up close next to him, saw the small flame that lay nestled in his palm.

"Where are we going?" asked Billy.

"Just follow me," replied Favian tersely. "Quietly."

They passed through the hallway and retraced their steps through the inn, down the narrow flight of stairs that led to the common room. At each creak, the woman flinched. When they arrived at the kitchen door, they halted.

"The common room is straight ahead," whispered Favian. "But if we try to leave the inn through the street door, we'll make a racket. It's heavily barred and bolted. The servants' entrance should be unlocked." He pointed toward the kitchen.

Elissa had no idea what the chance of one door being locked over another might be. However, if this kitchen was anything like the one in Bruno's Manor, it was likely to have a number of people sleeping by the hearth.

"There will be people inside," she whispered. "We need to find another way out."

Favian hesitated only a second. Then he beckoned for them to follow him back up to the second floor.

"The roofs all connect in this part of the city," Billy whispered once they had distanced themselves from the kitchen. Sure enough, once they had climbed the staircase to the top floor, they found themselves gazing over a sea of gray slate tiles. It would not be an easy escape, or a silent one. Favian was contemplating the risks when the sound of enraged cursing brought him to a decision.

Wordlessly, Favian held out his hands and

hoisted Elissa over the railing, setting her carefully down on the tiles. "Watch your step," he whispered.

Billy turned to the woman and simply lifted her in his arms. He didn't put her down, even after he'd climbed over the railing. Although he was carrying her weight, Billy was as sure-footed as a cat as he stepped over the tiles. Elissa had the strong feeling that he had done this sort of thing before. Elissa and Favian followed Billy along the ridge, feeling for toeholds. Fortunately, there was a row of flat tiles along the peak of the roof. It was very narrow, wide enough for only one foot, but if she held her arms out for balance, Elissa found she could walk upright.

I'm like one of those acrobats at the summer fair, she thought. *Only I don't know what I'm doing.* She tried not to think about the slippery, fog-drenched roof slanting down at a steep pitch just a few inches away from her feet. Elissa peered through the mist to the ground below. From three stories up, it was a long way down. She remembered the stones that lined the streets of Gravesport and knew that if anyone fell from this height, there would surely be broken bones.

They proceeded cautiously, but even so, the tiles rattled with their passage. It seemed to Elissa that with the noise they were making, the whole city should be sounding the alarm. She was sure that the villains who had tied Billy up would have no trouble finding their escape route.

No sooner had the idea crossed her mind than she heard the unmistakable sounds of pursuit. Whoever these men were, they weren't concerned about keeping quiet.

Elissa looked back over her shoulder. She couldn't see anybody coming behind them, but Favian had stopped. She hesitated.

"Keep going!" he hissed.

He turned around and headed back the way they had come.

"What are you doing?" Elissa called.

Favian either didn't hear her or didn't want to answer. He was busy prying up the flat tiles along the top of the roof. Oddly, he wasn't throwing them down but simply holding them in his hands and repositioning them. "Go!" he said. "I'll catch up to you."

Elissa didn't want to leave him behind, but she had no choice. Billy and the pale woman were well ahead of them by now. She stepped forward, keeping her eyes on the tiles. When she glanced back, she saw a faint reddish glow reflected across the shiny rooftop.

Soon she caught up with Billy. "Where's the Count?" he asked.

Elissa didn't have a chance to answer. The night was split by a high-pitched scream, then by another, followed by a scrabbling sound and one thud, then another. Then there was silence. Elissa smelled something acrid, like burning leather or flesh.

Within moments Favian appeared through the mist, a self-satisfied smile on his face.

"Did you? Are they?" Elissa didn't know quite what to say.

"I did, and they are," said Favian curtly. "Now, let's not dawdle. We still have to find a way down."

Down? Elissa looked over the edge of the roof. She thought of the two men who had slid off the tiles behind them and shuddered. "How?" asked Elissa.

"As soon as we get to a lower level," said Favian, "we'll jump."

"Jump?" said Elissa.

"Yes, jump," replied Favian. "Unless you would prefer to fly like your little feathered friends. No? I thought not."

Elissa clamped her mouth shut. He really was unbearable, and just when she had started to believe they might actually have something in common. All at once, she wanted to get as far away from Favian as possible.

"Let me go first," she said, inwardly fuming. Carefully, she inched her way around Billy and the woman until her view of the rooftops was unimpeded by pompous counts with their sarcastic little comments and their noses raised so high in the air that *they* should be the ones sprouting wings!

There was an adjoining roof up ahead. They could go right or stay on a straight course. She started to go straight. Almost immediately she felt a fluttering beside her ear.

"Go right," a small voice said.

Elissa did not question the instruction, for the moth had never steered her wrong before, although she did briefly wonder where her little guide had been hiding all this time. Certainly not in her hair, or she'd have felt it. Even so, the moth somehow always seemed close at hand when it was needed, making sure she went in the right direction.

"Well," hissed Favian, "are we going to wait here all night for you to make a decision? It's almost dawn."

Although the sky was still dark, Elissa sensed a faint lightening toward the east—the telltale blush that preceded dawn. Elissa cautiously turned to the right, and after a few yards she sensed the presence of four-legged creatures below. *Ah,* she thought. *Some* pleasant *company for a change.*

"There's a stable ahead," she said in a low voice. She continued on, and the rest had no choice but to follow her lead. Eventually the roof gave way to a lower roof. They clambered over the edge without mishap. Thankfully, Favian said nothing further to Elissa. She couldn't afford to let herself be distracted by his rudeness. It was taking all her concentration to keep from slipping on the slick tiles.

Soon the scent of hay and manure wafted up to them. "This is it," Elissa said softly. She had made her way gingerly to the lower edge of a roof overhanging a dark courtyard. It still looked like a long way to jump.

"There's usually a rainspout," offered Billy. "When I was a lad, I used to climb up ours all the time, though Mum always pitched a fit when she found out."

Elissa looked over the edge of the roof again. Indeed, there was a rainspout with a barrel at the end. The rainspout didn't look especially sturdy. She doubted it could support anybody's weight, let alone Billy's.

"It can't be more than seven or eight feet to the ground. I'll go down first," said Favian. He swung himself over the side of the roof with ease, grasped the spout, and slid down the remainder of the way. She heard his feet hit the cobblestones with a soft thud. Once on the ground, he raised his arms. "Just hang on to the edge of the roof and let go. I'll catch you."

Elissa eased herself over the edge. Favian caught her by the waist and immediately set her on her feet. She was grateful for the briefness of the contact, having no wish to be in his arms a second longer than she absolutely had to. Nor did Favian seem to wish to hold her there, for no sooner was Elissa upright than he raised his arms for the woman. Billy lowered her carefully. Then he climbed down the spout. Soon all four were standing side by side. The strong, comforting scent of the sleeping animals brought tears to Elissa's eyes. How she missed the uncomplicated ways of beasts!

They stood there together for a moment, catching their breath and assessing their whereabouts. They were standing in a large cobbled courtyard. At the rear was the stable. The outlines of several low gates were just discernible. A misty darkness obscured the rest of the courtyard.

"The door to the street should be that way." Favian extended his arm to indicate a vague space in front of them.

"Can we have some light?" requested Elissa, so softly that only Favian could hear her. At this point, she hated to ask him for anything, but the darkness was truly impenetrable. "We won't be able to find our way without it."

Favian didn't reply but merely raised his left hand high, revealing two doors—one wide, one narrow—in a building to their right. At that moment, the woman was positioned so that Favian's light fell directly upon her face. Elissa stared at her. Now that her downy hair had drifted back, she could see the woman's features quite clearly. She was, in fact, a young woman. And all of her was white—skin, eyebrows, even her eyes, which glowed a pale mother-of-pearl in Favian's light. The effect was unearthly; Elissa had never seen anyone like her. The pale woman did not seem to notice Elissa's scrutiny. Her gaze was fixed on the narrow door. She was already making her way toward it.

"Wait a moment—" Favian began.

He never had the chance to finish his warning. For just then the door burst open.

"Who goes there?" An enormous woman stood before them, blocking their way. It was clear she meant business, for she was aiming a knife expertly with one hand and brandishing a butcher's cleaver in the other. A smaller but equally threatening figure stood beside her, holding another weapon of some sort. Behind them both, yet another figure stood menacingly in the darkness.

"Don't!" cried Elissa. But it was too late. The woman had already thrown the knife. Favian felt the air move as it whizzed by his ear, striking the stable door with a resounding thwack. He raised his sword high and shouted.

All the commotion was apparently too much for the sleeping animals, for at Favian's cry a furious noise arose from the stable. A sharp crack, like the sound of hooves kicking open a stall, reverberated through the courtyard. A moment later, a dark animal emerged and made its way steadily toward them, braying.

"Gertrude!" exclaimed Elissa. She flew across the courtyard toward the stable.

"Elissa!" shouted Maya, dropping her rock. She ran past Favian in order to embrace Elissa, who, by now, had both arms wrapped about the donkey's neck.

"Mama!" yelled Billy.

"Where have you been?" asked Doc, coming through the doorway. "We've been waiting all night."

Favian couldn't help himself. He sank to the ground and began to laugh. As he sat convulsed on the cobblestones, holding his heaving sides, the light went out, leaving them all in the dark.

Clutching Gertrude's fuzzy neck with both

hands, Elissa could not help but laugh herself, out of sheer joy. But she swallowed her laughter when she felt something large draw close to her in the darkness. When it was almost upon her, it breathed heavily in her ear.

"What's the joke?" said Ralph.

The Windsinger's Tale

In the lonely hour just before dawn, the damp sea mist lay like a clammy sheet over the city of Gravesport. Lily's kitchen, however, was warm and cozy and ahum with soft voices. A fire was blazing in the hearth, over which hung an ancient black kettle that, at the moment, was whistling urgently. Lily's guests sat comfortably around the kitchen fire, nursing mugs of steaming tea. Favian, as always, sat with his back to the hearth, keeping his eye on the doors. There were two to keep track of—one to the courtyard and one to the common room—so he had placed himself where he could watch them both. Doc had located himself near the stairway, "keeping an ear unfurled" for the Captain in case he woke up. Elissa sat next to Maya, with Gertrude behind her, breathing moistly down her neck. In spite of Lily's protests, Gertrude had entered the kitchen hot on Elissa's heels, and once reunited with Elissa the donkey could not be moved. Ralph, on the other hand, had yawned and, after greeting Elissa cordially, ambled back to his stall. The kitchen was ample, cheerful, and spotless.

Lily kept a wary eye on the donkey. "She'd better not crap on my floor," she said.

"Don't worry. She knows better," Elissa reassured her. Nevertheless, Elissa grabbed the donkey and threw her arm around her neck. Only Maya heard her whisper something into the donkey's ear. Gertrude snorted and stamped her hoof in protest. Then, reluctantly, she backed herself up until she was halfway through the doorway. Once in that position, with her hindquarters hanging out into the courtyard but her front hooves and head still in the kitchen, she stared at Lily, as if to say, *Is that good enough for you?*

"That's better," hmphed Lily. She was not even remotely put off by the donkey's baleful eye as she passed around a basket of sweet buns and breakfast rolls. "Here, Maya," she said, handing the girl a bun sprinkled with cinnamon and sugar. Lily had taken a shine to the child, not having had any girls of her own. Billy looked flabbergasted.

"And me thinkin' Maya was yer mum this whole time!" exclaimed Billy.

"No," said Elissa, surprised. "I don't have a mother."

Lily clucked her tongue in sympathy. "Poor motherless child," she muttered. "Wandering thither and yon with the likes o' this bunch." She cuffed Billy for good measure and reached into the basket to fish out a plump, warm bun, which she passed to Elissa.

Elissa didn't eat it right away but cradled it in her hands, thinking. "How did you end up here?" she asked Maya over the hubbub. And then, in a whisper, "How did *Ralph* get here?"

Maya squirmed in delight. "Oh, that's the best part!" she whispered. "It was a complete *ac cident*! Somebody bought him in Alhamazar to sell to some noble here, and Lily has the best stable in town. So . . ." Maya bit a chunk out of her bun. "Mmmm."

Elissa didn't really believe that Ralph had

been put up for sale. Knowing Ralph, he had probably "wandered off," hot on Gertrude's trail, and someone with a lack of scruples had taken advantage of the situation. "And you?" Elissa prompted.

"Oh," said Maya, "Captain Jarvison is a friend of Lily's. He brought us here after we landed. He said her boardinghouse would be safer than an inn."

Elissa nodded. She had a vague memory of Billy mentioning "old Jarvey" in connection with his "mum." At the time, however, she'd had too much on her mind to pay close attention.

Maya's chin began to quiver. "Oh, I was so worried about you!" she cried. "I thought I'd never see you again! Where did you *go?*"

Elissa wiped a tear from Maya's cheek. "I'm so sorry," she said. Sheepishly, she described her shopping adventure in Alhamazar. "It was very foolish of me," she said. Suddenly Elissa struck herself on the forehead. For the life of her, she couldn't remember what she'd done with the packet of silk.

"What is it?" asked Maya.

"All that trouble for a length of silk, and I've lost it!" she said.

"No, you haven't," said Doc. "You left it aboard the *Maiden*. I always wondered what was in that package."

Elissa blushed. "I guess I was distracted," she said. Maya laughed through her tears and hugged Elissa close.

"I'll get it if you like," said Doc. A few minutes later he returned with the packet under his arm. Elissa took it from him with a grateful smile and handed it to Maya.

As the silk spilled out of its oilcloth wrapper, Maya gasped, "It's beautiful!" They all drew close to admire it, uttering soft aahs of appreciation. Even Favian left his post by the hearth. He regarded the shimmering cloth with a puzzled look.

"But how on earth did you find *us*?" said Maya.

Elissa looked at Billy, who shifted uncomfortably in his chair. "I swear, Mama must have moved . . ."

Lily stopped kneading her dough long enough

to give Billy an incredulous look. "Moved! Like I don't know where me own home is!" she cried. "It's forty-five years I've lived here. An' I borned this one right here, in this very kitchen! Whilst I was stirring the pudding! And nary a lump in it!" She cuffed Billy lightly behind his ear with a floury hand. He gazed at her adoringly.

"Mum never gets lost. She was a navigator b'fore she opened the stable," he said proudly. "So was her pappy before her. Runs in the family."

Thinking of Billy's sense of direction, or lack thereof, Elissa very much doubted that. She also doubted she could adequately answer Maya's question. How *did* she get here? The whole trip seemed so unbelievable. However, she tried gamely to explain, starting from their separation in Alhamazar. Favian interjected with his story at the appropriate time. But when they came to the previous evening's rescue, Elissa fell silent. She looked about the kitchen. Where was the pale woman?

In a corner of the room, the woman sat crouched on the floor, her arms protectively encircling her knees. She looked, for all the world, like a statue made of snow.

Elissa gestured for her to come closer. "You are among friends," she said. "Don't worry, no one will harm you here."

The woman slowly stood and approached the group. Now that it was morning, Elissa could see the true color of her eyes. Last night she had thought they were mother-of-pearl, but now she could see they were as clear as glass. No, not clear—they were like mirrors, reflecting and refracting the light in subtle, ever-changing patterns. Now they reflected the hues of the morning sky, but underneath those subtle gray mists, Elissa could make out clouds billowing against a vivid blue sky as they flowed and changed with the wind. The effect was hypnotic. Elissa stood and took her by the hand. It lay gently in hers, as light as a feather.

"Come sit," Elissa said, drawing the pale woman to a stool. The woman sank down, obviously exhausted. Lily passed her a mug, which she took in her hands. She did not lift it to her pale lips—perhaps she did not have the strength.

Elissa contemplated the woman's faraway expression, realizing that she knew nothing about her. She did not even know her name. Under the circumstances, she was not sure she should ask; the woman still looked so frightened. Elissa thought that maybe the woman would feel more at ease if she knew who they all were.

"I am Elissa, of High Crossing," she said softly. "This is my friend Maya, and that is Gertrude." Maya smiled, and Gertrude nodded from the doorway. The pale woman looked up.

"You have already met Favian," Elissa continued. Favian stood and bowed briefly, then mumbled something, but without his usual flourish. His rapt contemplation of Gertrude's gray snout had been interrupted. There was a somewhat distracted expression on his face, as though he were recalling something bothersome. Gertrude swished her tail at him.

When Elissa turned to Doc, he gave the pale woman an interested nod. "Everyone calls me Doc," he said. "I don't know why."

Lily wiped her hands on a towel and patted Doc affectionately on his grizzled head. "Yer called *Dock*," she said with emphasis. "Because yer old and gray and full o' splinters."

Doc said, "Get on with you," but he winked at Lily when he thought nobody else was looking.

Elissa, smiling, continued with her introductions. "This is Lily. And you've met her son, Billy."

Billy nodded, speechless, his eyes glued to the pale woman's face. He had never in his whole life seen anything more beautiful. The woman had looked at each one of them as they were introduced, her eyes changing, unreadable. But when she looked at Billy, there was a message in her eyes—a message for him.

The woman was saying something.

Elissa leaned forward expectantly. Nevertheless, the words floated past her ears, with no more substance than a sigh. She couldn't catch anything. "Aieesh?" repeated Elissa.

The group had fallen silent in order to better hear the woman's breathy voice.

"Aesha," repeated the woman. "Aesha Windsinger."

"Oh," cried Lily, dropping her serving spoon on the gray flagstone floor. At the sudden clatter, they all jumped.

Billy reached down to pick it up. "I told yer," he said quietly as he handed it to Lily. "Didn't I tell yer there was still some left? Didn't I, Doc?"

Aesha had watched the exchange, her eyes fathomless. "Only one," she affirmed. "After me, there will be no more." The group sat silent, waiting for her to continue. She closed her eyes and began to speak, reciting her story in a singsong voice, as though she had told it a hundred times before.

"We are the Windsingers," she chanted. "Our home is the Great Circle, where the wind always sings."

Elissa was awed. Her mother's people had wandered throughout the Far North, yet she would venture to say that none of them had traveled as far as the Great Circle. No one had ever climbed those remote mountains. They held up the sky. But in all the stories Nana had told her, she had never once mentioned Windsingers.

"We lived on the Mountain, all alone, until a traveler came among us. One of our young ones found him lost in the snows, nearly dead from the cold. We took him into our dwelling and cared for him. We sang our songs for him, and breathed our breath into him, until he was strong. And then he spoke to us. He spoke of broad plains and vast seas. He spoke of new winds—new songs."

Aesha paused. "He had a hairy face and a hungry look in his eyes, which we did not understand. When we sang for him, he said, 'Beautiful, beautiful,' but he did not look happy. When the traveler departed, the young ones went with him, to explore the places beyond our mountains, to hear the winds sing over the seas and the plains. He promised they would return, but we never saw our young ones again. More of us left the Circle to find the ones who had wandered away. Our chorus became so small, we could no longer sing the Great Song."

Elissa did not quite understand what Aesha meant by "the Great Song," but she did not want to interrupt the Windsinger's tale. Aesha's voice, while thin, had a haunting quality to it, like the sound of a far-off flute. The longer Elissa listened, the more the sound captivated her, drawing her in. She could listen to it all day.

"My mother and I left. We hoped to find our lost kin and bring them home. We left the elders behind. They had no desire to leave. Their spirits, they said, would not accompany them, and what good was a body devoid of spirit? So they remained to die alone, unsung." Aesha bowed her head sadly. "It was a long difficult journey across the lowlands. We grew heavy. After many weeks, we were found by sea people who took us onto their boats. They bid us sing for them, and they gave us silver and gold. We had no use for the coins, so we flung them into the sea." Aesha stopped to take a breath. It was clear that speaking at such great length was difficult for her.

"Yer threw gold into the sea?" asked Billy, incredulous.

"Yes, we did," whispered Aesha. "Then, when they told us not to, we put the coins into a bag. They were too heavy to carry. My mother began to weaken. We had not found any of our kin, and her spirit became weak, so far away from our mountains. After she faded away, I was alone. My voice left me. I wanted to return to my home, to find my voice again. I used the bag of coins to buy my passage north. The men took my gold and my silver willingly. Then they caged me. They tried to make me sing for them, but I could not. When they tired of beating me and starving me, they sold me. They sold me many times, until finally the one-eyed man brought me here. He said his Master had ways to make me sing." Aesha shivered and looked about, as if searching for something in the shadows. "He is an evil man."

There was silence in the room. Elissa was horrified at the abuse the poor woman had suffered. Still, there was something she could not fathom. She could not understand why seafarers would hire a woman to sing for them. "What songs do you sing?" she asked.

"I sing Windsong," said Aesha simply. "When my people sing, the wind sings with us."

Doc nodded. "There's captains would pay a fortune for her," he said. "Your sails would never hang empty, and you'd be able to travel anywhere, anytime. Fast."

Elissa shook her head in wonder. "You mean, you can make the wind blow?"

Aesha cocked her head to the side and held it there in a curious angular pose. She smiled. "Our song *is* the wind. When we sing, our voices move all around us. Many voices, one song, all together." Aesha's face shone briefly with a deep inner glow. She released her breath in a long, slow sigh, and the glow disappeared. "I must return to my home," she said. "To join my spirit to the Great Wind."

Elissa looked around the room. As her gaze lingered on Favian, Aesha, and Maya, their faces bathed in hearthlight, an odd feeling flickered through her. She was on the verge of realizing something very important. But before she could grasp it, the revelation slipped away, leaving her with the uncomfortable feeling that she was holding all the pieces of a puzzle but had no idea where to put them. It had been a very long night, and she was having problems thinking.

"You'll go home," promised Elissa. "I will find a way." She yawned. "But right now, I need to go to bed."

After taking a long nap, Elissa found it easier to assess their situation. She decided that the best course of action would be to go directly to Castlemar. Taking Aesha to her father's holdings, even if he wasn't actually there, was more practical than trying to get her home from Suleskerry, wherever that might be. At least Castlemar lay to the north. Opening her pack, which Maya had brought with her from Jarvison's boat, she found her old cloak. Briefly, she held the rough, familiar cloth against her face and breathed in the scent of home. With a little sigh, she laid it across her knees and ripped open the corner of the hem. With her thumb, she eased out a gold coin. *There's only one left now,* she thought. *Nana would surely scold me if she knew how fast I was spending her money.* Then she plopped the coin into her purse and set out for the wharves with the intention of booking passage. She'd told Favian she wanted to buy some new boots, which was plausible, as the soles were wearing thin. Even though she hated lying, it was just too problematic to explain why she needed to go to Castlemar. If she did, then she'd have to tell him about her father, and she was sure he'd never believe her. In a way, she had been very dishonest, traveling with Doc and Billy and Favian all this time as if she were just a humble peasant girl. Now she wasn't quite sure how to rectify things. She'd have to ask Maya when she woke up.

* * *

But for all her resolve, by late afternoon Elissa found herself gazing out at the gray sea, discouraged and weary. Initially, she had thought it would be easy to find a passenger ship—there were so many ships scattered about in the harbor, although most looked as if they had been anchored there for a while. Only one ship seemed to be a recent arrival. As she walked down the wharf, a sleek galleon was just lowering her sails. From the top of the mast, a flag with royal insignia still waved, signaling the arrival of a visiting dignitary. While there was absolutely no chance of traveling aboard that ship, Elissa thought she might be able to find passage on one of the cargo ships. With their bare masts pointing up at the sky, most of them looked like they were due for a voyage.

Elissa walked up to the first of the ramshackle offices that flanked the docks in a long, uneven line. Attached to the door was a weathered sign depicting a ship in full sail. She knocked and the door swung open.

Inside the office, a gnarled man was sitting at a blocky desk, smoking a pipe. He had propped his feet on the desk, which, considering the piles of debris that lay cast about haphazardly on the greasy floor planks, was probably the best place to put them. The place reeked of rotting fish.

"Tarbuckle Enterprises," growled the man. "What do you want?"

"Are you Captain Tarbuckle?" she inquired. The man didn't answer, which flustered Elissa. "I would like to book passage aboard a ship bound for Castlemar," she said.

The man looked Elissa up and down before spitting copiously on the floor. "What's the matter, lass? Your boyfriend join the King's Navy and leave you with child?"

He had the habit of talking around his pipe so that when he spoke, he revealed his cracked yellow teeth in a sort of sneer.

"Certainly not!" said Elissa, scandalized. "I'm traveling with three companions and some, uh— some livestock."

"Sounds like a circus," he scoffed. "Well, boyfriend or village fair, it hardly matters to me. The voyage is too dangerous at this time of year." Tarbuckle's grimy boots remained firmly planted on his desk as he addressed her, concretely demonstrating his complete unwillingness to travel. "Wait a month for the spring storms to pass." He shoved the pipe farther into his mouth. "And don't listen to anyone who tells you otherwise," he added.

Elissa looked out the dirt-caked window at the calm gray sky. "It doesn't seem stormy," she observed.

"Maybe it does, maybe it doesn't," said Tarbuckle in a bored voice.

"I can pay you now," said Elissa, remembering Doc's pronouncement that people would do anything for gold. She felt for her purse, which lay with reassuring heaviness around her neck.

Tarbuckle hesitated. "How much?" He narrowed his eyes shrewdly under a set of bushy eyebrows. This was the response that Elissa had been waiting for.

"Gold," she said without hesitation.

Tarbuckle let out a huge guffaw, nearly losing his pipe in the process. It was a good thing he had it glued to his lips, because Elissa imagined that if it dropped to the floor, he might never find it again.

"Wench," he wheezed, "even if I believed you,

what good would your gold do me at the bottom of the sea?"

Elissa tried to protest, but Tarbuckle waved dismissively toward his office door, still chuckling. He hadn't moved his feet an inch.

Elissa continued down the docks, poking her head into one grimy office after another, only to be told the same thing. "Wait," they all said. "About a month." Elissa didn't want to wait. She wanted to get to Castlemar—soon.

There was only one alternative. She would have to return to Tarbuckle Enterprises. The other captains had informed her that if Tarbuckle refused to sail north, it was for good reason. Elissa reflected that at least Tarbuckle had *given* her a reason. None of the others had even bothered, although one of them had offered her some kind of "insurance" should she manage to find an outbound ship. And when she'd mentioned Suleskerry—since going south was better than staying in Gravesport—they had laughed, as if this were the funniest thing they'd ever heard.

However, Elissa had another, even more pressing motivation for returning to Tarbuckle

Enterprises—for, unbelievably, his was the cleanest of all the offices she had seen that day. She felt that, comparatively speaking, this did much to recommend him.

So Elissa returned to Tarbuckle's office, resolved to try again. From the position of Tarbuckle's pipe and feet, it appeared that he had not moved since she last saw him.

"You don't give up easily, do you?" he growled.

"No, I don't." Elissa tapped her foot. She was losing patience. "What's the real reason you won't take me?"

Tarbuckle removed his pipe. "Pirates!" he barked, making Elissa jump. "They're all waiting like vultures out there. Do you think I'd risk my ship, my crew, my cargo, and my life for the sake of a pleasure cruise?"

"It's not a pleasure cruise," said Elissa defensively. "I have to get home."

"Well, my girl, try walking. There's not a ship in this harbor will set sail for you." The man leaned back in his chair again, satisfied that he had made his point.

"How about the ship that just arrived?" Elissa

felt that a challenge was in order. It seemed impossible to her that not a single captain was willing to leave the harbor.

"That's different," he said. "Even pirates know better than to attack the Royal Navy." The man suddenly guffawed again. "That's the ticket! Go ask the King if you can hitch a ride with him. Tell him you'll pay him in gold!" This time Tarbuckle laughed until the pipe *did* fall from his mouth. He didn't bother to pick it up. "No, here's a better one," he called as she strode toward the door. "Tell him you're a princess and he'll take you for free!"

"Disagreeable old coot," she muttered as she stomped her way down the pier. Maybe she *should* walk to Castlemar. After all, she had walked to Gravesport—with a little assistance from Gertrude, Ralph, and the *Swamp Maiden*. By the time she reached the end of the pier, Elissa was in such a state of frustration, she imagined she might actually be capable of walking straight across the sea. However, once the bleached, wind-roughened boards stopped, she had to stop as well—or sink into the oily gray waves. With all the ships moored solidly in the harbor, Elissa was faced with the possibility of a long stay in this dismal city. Behind her rose the gray buildings, above her hung the gray sky, before her stretched the gray ocean. Even the gulls looked unhappy here.

Elissa stood looking out over the sea. In her palm, the gold coin that was to have served as her passage home lay as useless as a plug of lead. She looked accusingly at the coin.

"No matter how far I travel," she said to the waves, "I can't seem to get anywhere. At the rate I'm going, I'll never find Falk." She sighed. "He probably thinks I'm dead by now."

She held Nana's coin up against the sky. When she had given Elissa the three gold coins—it seemed a lifetime had passed since that day—Nana had said, "The world awaits." Elissa straightened her shoulders.

Not long ago she'd been penniless, lost, and alone in Alhamazar. She might be stuck in Gravesport, but at least she had friends—and gold. This wasn't a disaster; it was just a setback. If she'd gotten this far, she'd find a way out. Elissa tossed the coin in the air, where it glinted in what little light remained of the day; then, deftly plucking it from its trajectory toward the deep waters, she plopped it into her purse.

Well, if her money would not suffice to buy sea passage, it would just have to serve for other things. She smiled, a bit wickedly, anticipating the stunned expression on Favian's face when she got back. He needed to be humbled. It would serve him right, after the way he had belittled her up on the rooftop. Then she headed back to the wharves, to the inn at the far end, where a beautiful brown-eyed maiden sat upon a rock.

∽ 16 ∾

Unanswered Questions

Favian paced the courtyard. He had been pacing for over an hour. For him, the afternoon was passing excruciatingly slowly. Ever since Elissa had left, Favian had been in an abysmal mood. Why was she so stubborn? He had given her a direct command not to go into the city, and she had ignored him completely.

"Boots?" he'd said, unable to believe his ears. "Can't they wait?"

"No," she'd answered, in that impertinent way of hers.

"You can't go by yourself," he had stated.

"And why not?" she had asked.

"The city is dangerous, especially with those ruffians on the loose." He had explained this very clearly to her. "I must accompany you."

"I don't need you. Aesha does. If the one-eyed man finds out she's here, she'll need you to defend her. You know the Captain and Doc won't be able to. And Billy isn't even here. He's probably gotten lost somewhere. Who knows when he'll be back?" Elissa whipped her desert robe around her. "Besides, I'll be disguised," she said. She pinned the robe shut and drew the hood down so it covered her face. Favian thought she would stick out like a sore thumb on the wharves, but he had to agree that at least she wouldn't be recognized—by the one-eyed man or anyone else.

As she stood solidly in front of him, he realized that Elissa could not be moved. "I can see where that . . . animal gets it from," he muttered.

"Gertrude," corrected Elissa. "Her name is Gertrude."

Remembering their conversation, Favian once again felt irritated—at her, but mostly at himself. All his encounters with Elissa made him feel powerless—foolish, even. As a member of a noble household, he was accustomed to asking questions, getting answers, giving orders, getting results. Perhaps that could be considered high-handed, but sometimes—often, in fact—people simply needed to do as they were told. But Elissa ... Elissa utterly confounded him. She looked like a simple farm girl, yet she was completely impervious to his rank and position. Moreover, she'd slipped into her role as "Contessa" entirely too easily. There was a mystery about her that he simply could not solve. It niggled at him like a splinter.

But the worst of it was that she had caught him off guard, forcing him to behave abominably. She probably thought he was an ill-mannered, arrogant lout. And if she did, she would be right. He was insufferable. Why had he mocked her so? For all the mystery surrounding her, he had to confess that Elissa had at least been honest. She'd been telling the truth about that donkey, for instance.

He hated to admit it, but he probably should apologize to her. Here, it was simple, common ways that mattered—truth, honesty, sincerity—not clever insults, political maneuvers, or betrayals, which, he had to admit, had only served to get his brothers killed and himself exiled.

Favian stopped pacing for a moment, coming

to a realization. The problem with Elissa was that she had *not* betrayed him. Apart from his mother, Elissa was the only person who knew about his power over fire. All his life, he had striven to protect that secret. It was the thing that marked him as different from others, but more than that, it was something that in this world of rivalry and suspicion might give others an excuse to destroy him. Yet Elissa had not used her knowledge against him. And now he was completely at her mercy. It was unsettling—frightening, even— and yet appealing, in an odd way. Why had she protected him?

Unanswered questions bothered Favian. They forced him to stop and think. He hated thinking. He'd much rather be *doing* something. He looked around for someone to talk to, but Billy had gone off earlier on a mysterious errand of his own and the little girl, Maya, was busy helping in the kitchen. Lily clearly did not want him underfoot. He suspected she did not like to be reminded of the fact that she'd almost skewered him with a carving knife that morning.

He decided to go visit the Captain. Doc had

given him the impression this morning that the Captain might be ready for a conversation in the afternoon if he hadn't "kicked the bucket" yet.

Favian climbed the staircase to the small room above the kitchen where the Captain was lodged and rapped on the door somewhat impatiently. When he realized he was knocking on the door of a man who was recovering from a grave injury, he knocked again, more softly this time.

"It's Favian," he called.

The door opened just a crack.

"Come in," said Doc. "He's awake."

Favian entered the room, which, though small, was neat as a pin. The room was lit by one small window, under which was a splay-legged table bearing a lantern and a basket of silk flowers. Beside the table was a large chair in which it appeared Doc had recently been sitting, for a coverlet had been thrown messily across the back. There was an open book resting on the arm. Next to the chair was a bed heaped high with quilts and blankets—Lily's work, no doubt. Left to his own devices, the Captain would have been content with a plank for a bed and a burlap sack for a cover. Favian could just make out the bristly graying beard of the Captain poking above the bedding. Wordlessly, Doc gestured for Favian to sit, pointing to the chair by the bed.

Favian sat down, unsure of how to begin. He wanted to know more about the cargo the Captain had delivered but realized it wouldn't be courteous to jump right into an interrogation. He imagined what Elissa might say, how she might behave, her sincerity.

"How are you feeling?" he asked.

"Oh, I'll be up and about in no time," said the Captain. His voice was weak. "Takes more than a bolt of lightning to keep me down."

Favian nodded, agreeing completely with the Captain's self-assessment.

"I'm sorry I put ye and the wee lass in danger," continued the Captain.

Favian reached over and touched the Captain lightly on the arm. "We are all in this together," he said. There was an uncomfortable moment of silence, which Favian broke by withdrawing something from his tunic. He held it out for the Captain to see.

"This is the weapon they used against you," said Favian.

"Evil-looking thing," said the Captain.

Favian placed the cylinder in the Captain's right hand.

"Have you seen anything like it before?" asked Favian. "Did you take a look inside any of those sacks you were delivering?"

"They pay, I deliver," the Captain said. "I don't ask any questions. And I don't investigate the goods." He turned the cylinder over in his hand. "But I can tell ye one thing. If these were aboard my *Maidie,* they weren't all she was carrying. Some of those sacks left a kind of sooty powder behind—like charcoal."

Favian pursed his lips. "It must be related somehow."

"Could be," said the Captain noncommittally. "But those sacks are long gone now, so we'll never know." He handed the cylinder back to Favian.

Doc cleared his throat. "Count," he said, "you might want to take a look at this." He held his palm out to Favian. In it rested a small pellet. "Bella took this out of Cappy's shoulder," he explained.

Favian looked at the pellet. It was obviously some form of projectile. Clearly, it was this small lump of metal that had done the damage to Cappy's shoulder, not fire. This could complicate matters. Favian had no power over projectiles.

"Whoever is making this weapon is going to have quite an advantage over everyone else," he said.

"How so?" asked Doc. "There are other weapons that can kill from a distance—arrows, catapults."

"It's the principle of the thing," explained Favian, raising the cylinder and running a finger along it to demonstrate his point. "With a longer cylinder, the pellets will travel a greater distance, much farther than an arrow can reach. And with a wider barrel, the size of the pellets can be increased, causing more damage. And unlike a catapult, this can be aimed with precision." He turned the cylinder thoughtfully in his hands. "The most dangerous thing about these is that they seem rather effortless to use. All you have to do is load them, ignite them somehow—perhaps with that black powder—and bang!"

Doc nodded wisely, and somewhat sadly. "So now there will be a race to see who gets them first."

"Exactly," said Favian. "Although I imagine the person who bought your cargo will have the advantage."

They fell silent for a moment.

"Can I keep the pellet?" Favian asked the Captain.

"Take it, if it will do ye some good." The Captain regarded Favian. "All in all, yer not a bad lad," he said. "In spite of yer upbringing."

Favian rose to leave, but the Captain held up his hand. "Thank ye, Count, for saving my life," he said. "I'll never forget it."

Favian looked down at the Captain as he lay swathed in bandages. Not too long ago, he would have accepted the gratitude with an ironic flourish—graciousness mixed with scorn. Today he held his hand out for the Captain to grasp.

"I know you won't," he said. Then he turned to leave, thinking that it was a pity he hadn't known more men like the Captain and Doc in his life.

"Oh, and I'd be keepin' an eye on the wee lass,"

called the Captain as Favian walked to the door. "She's got hidden talents. Heard she can pick a lock like a pro." The Captain gave Favian a broad wink.

"I'll be careful." Favian's tone was mock-serious, though privately he wondered what other "talents" she had hidden from him.

Favian made his way down the stairs. Almost instantly he felt a need to be out in the open. He passed through the doorway into the courtyard, where he could pace freely.

What was she *doing* all this time?

Favian snapped his fingers against the hilt of his sword. A spark flew out and fell slowly to the cobblestones. He stopped his pacing to grind the ember out with his foot. It seemed that ever since he'd met Elissa, he had been spouting fire. When she returned, he meant to get some answers—as was his due.

It completely slipped Favian's mind that not too long ago he had simply intended to apologize.

Elissa entered the common room just as Lily was setting out the table and chairs. When she saw Elissa, Lily jerked her head expressively toward the courtyard. "*His Highness* has been waiting," she said.

Elissa proceeded to the courtyard, where lanterns had already been lit and where Favian clearly had been pacing. There was a line of soot on the cobblestones. Favian whirled around to face her.

"Where have you been?" he hissed. "It's almost dark."

Wordlessly, Elissa dropped a small object into his hand. It gleamed dark red in the center of his palm. Favian stared at it, speechless. He opened his mouth, but Elissa spoke first.

"Your stone was worth far more than the price of supper and two beds," she said. She couldn't help sounding smug. The look on his face was worth a *hundred* pieces of gold.

Elissa tried to angle past him.

"Wait!" he cried.

Elissa raised her eyebrows. Now that she had the advantage, she was not about to lose it.

"Where did you get the money?" he asked lamely.

"It was given to me when I left home," she said. "Are you not pleased?"

"Yes, of course I am . . . ," he stammered. He stiffened his spine and cleared his throat, holding up a hand to get her attention. Elissa beat him to it.

"Do you want to explain about last night?" she asked. "I know you can make fire with your hands." There was no point hiding what they both knew. Besides, she had a Gift as well. In spite of her resolve to hold her ground, Elissa dropped her head, realizing that she hadn't exactly been honest with Favian. But what did that matter? He was hardly interested in anything she had to say. She looked up to meet his gaze. His eyes flashed red.

"You have gold to spend, the finest piece of silk I've ever seen, and you don't seem to care a whit about my rank. Who are you, really? Once and for all," Favian demanded, "I think I am entitled to—"

Elissa interrupted him. "No," she said firmly. "You are titled, not *en*titled. There is a big difference." She stood before him, her hands on her hips, looking for all the world like a mother scolding her child.

Favian stared at her as if he had been slapped. In a way, he had been. No one had ever spoken to him like that before. His mind reeled, and then—gradually, like the sun rising over the horizon—the full import of what she had said struck home. He had no rights over her. It was she who had power over him—the power of generosity. Elissa had saved his life and discovered his secret. Yet unlike himself, she had never tried to use her power against anyone. As he finally absorbed what she had been saying all along—with words, with deeds, with her very nature—the terrible burden of entitlement lifted from his shoulders.

"Please . . . ," he said quietly. "Please tell me the truth."

She wasn't prepared for "please." Not for the request, or for the expression that had come over his face. For the first time since she had known him, he looked open, sincere, completely vulnerable. He was asking her for honesty. Elissa felt as though she were on the brink of something big—even bigger than when Maya had discovered her Gift, for now there was so much more to reveal. Perhaps it would not be such a terrible risk. Maya had guessed Elissa's secret, and, if anything, they were closer for having shared their

Gifts. Favian also had a Gift. And aside from his lapses into being a royal pain, he was not a coward or dishonest. It was time she revealed her true self as well. She needed to tell him about her Gift—about Gertrude and . . . everything.

Elissa took a deep breath. And froze.

Both Elissa and Favian turned toward the door simultaneously as Lily's voice boomed from deep within the confines of the house. "I tells ye, we've no young missy staying here. This is a stable."

Another voice, pitched low, answered her. Elissa could not make out the words, but they sounded insistent.

"No, ye cannot search, I don't care who ye be!" cried Lily. There was the bark of a command, the squeak of a table and chairs being shoved aside, the tramp of boots, Lily's cry for help.

Favian grabbed Elissa by the hand. They were both thinking the same thing: the one-eyed man.

"Quickly!" he whispered. "You run up the stairs and wake Aesha. Get her out—over the roof if you have to. I'll stay here and deal with them." Favian drew his sword. "Go!"

"No," said Elissa, pulling at his arm. "I won't go unless you come with me." However competent a swordsman Favian might be, she was not about to leave him to the one-eyed man and his gang of cutthroats. She was sure they would show Favian no mercy.

"You *never* listen to me!" he cried, trying to shake off her hand. "You are going to get us *both* killed!"

Elissa continued to tug at him. "Not if you come with me."

With a twist and a vigorous shake, Favian freed himself from Elissa and tried to push her toward the stairway. However, it was already too late. A man burst into the courtyard, flanked by several fully armed soldiers.

Grabbing Elissa, Favian raised his sword and prepared to attack, but to his utter dismay Elissa would not stay behind him. Instead, she ran forward, her arms reaching toward the dark stranger, who was lifting his hand—

"Elissa, no!" Favian howled. "Stop!"

"Father!" she cried.

The man who had entered the courtyard, and who now held Elissa in his arms, wore purple robes over his mail and a golden crown upon his head. On either side of him, guards bearing the insignia of the Royal House of Castlemar arrayed themselves at the ready. Favian stood frozen for a second or two, in a state of complete stupefaction. Then, lowering his head and sword, he dropped to one knee. At last his questions had been answered—once and for all.

∽ 17 ∾

The King of Castlemar

It had all happened so fast—the tramp of boots, the guards all around, and that brief illuminated moment in which Elissa recognized Falk's narrow face. The word had burst from Elissa's lips, and then, before she knew it, she was in his arms. It was only when he was holding her against his breast that she realized he had never touched her before, let alone held her, and that she had never called him "Father." Elissa took in Falk's scent— leather and steel. It was wholly unfamiliar to her. She drew back a bit, and he let her go.

"Let me look at you," he said.

Elissa was reluctant, unsure of what she might see in his face once she had achieved a certain distance. She took a step or two away from him, then lifted her head. Except for the crown and the robes, Falk looked very much as he had the last time she had seen him: the same haughty, high-bridged nose bending down to a fine aristocratic mouth; the same sharp, observant eyes—the face of command. But there was something new in his expression as he gazed at her—pride.

"You have grown," he said, smiling.

She smiled back, seeking warmth.

Falk took Elissa's hand and drew her beside him.

"Rise," he said to the young man who had knelt before him. Favian rose at Falk's command while Falk examined him.

In spite of Falk's close scrutiny Favian remained tall and erect. Elissa knew, from personal experience, how difficult that particular feat was. She had to admire Favian for not wilting. In his shabby clothes and travel-worn cloak, he faced Falk without so much as a tremor. Grasping the hilt of his sword, Favian stood at the ready. Elissa glanced at Falk. Though his face bore its habitually stern expression, his eyes twinkled. In some strange, inexplicable way, Elissa felt pleased. Falk gave Favian permission to introduce himself.

"Favian, Count of Leonne," he said steadily.

Falk nodded. "I knew your father. Your young brothers are making a royal mess of Leonne. It's about time you were reinstated."

Favian's jaw dropped.

"We'll talk about it later," said Falk. "Now let us dine. I am famished." He gestured for Favian to accompany them and started to pass back through the wide common room door.

"Wait!" cried Elissa. She held out her hand to block Falk from passing through the doorway. When she was sure he had halted, she poked her head inside. Sure enough, Lily was there. "He's my father," she whispered. She never imagined she'd be saying those words in a Gravesport stableyard. In fact, she hardly believed them herself.

At the words "He's my father," Falk blinked and then pressed his eyes shut for just a moment.

Elissa motioned for Falk to enter. As expected, Lily stood blocking the entryway. She'd obviously made a detour through the kitchen. In her right hand she held a massive butcher knife, and in her left something that looked like a meat skewer.

It seemed to Elissa that Falk gave Lily an approving look. "Has dinner been served?" he asked innocently.

The belligerence slowly drained from Lily's face. She gestured toward the common room with her knife. "It's stew tonight." She considered her guest for a moment and added grudgingly, "An' dumplins, seeing as you're 'Lissa's dad." She turned her head away from them and bellowed, "It's all right," into the common room. Then, with the point of her blade, she waved them inside.

Falk adjusted the crown on his head and, with Elissa on his right and Favian on his left, entered the common room with all the dignity that circumstances would allow.

The room, which had been empty when Elissa returned from the docks, was now full. Elissa looked at Falk as he swept his eyes around the room, studying its occupants, sizing them up. She knew what he was seeing: a wide-shouldered young sailor, a grizzled old man, a girl with liquid brown eyes, and a pale, slender woman. Eventually, she hoped, he would see them as she did:

loyal comrades all. Billy hovered protectively over Aesha, whose timeless eyes reflected the dusk. Maya gazed steadfastly at Elissa, ready to come to her aid. Doc appeared to be dozing by the fire, though Elissa suspected he was not asleep.

"Perhaps you remember Maya," said Elissa as the small girl rose to her feet. "Maya helped me escape from the Citadel," she added. Falk nodded graciously to the young girl and thanked her.

"And this is Aesha," continued Elissa. The pale creature unfolded herself from her seat, rising slowly until she stood at her full height. Falk nodded again.

Elissa held out her hand. "This is Billy, Lily's son. You've, um, met Lily," she added softly. Falk smiled and performed a stiff mock salute to the sailor, whose cheerful freckled face broke into a broad grin.

"And this is Doc." The old man cocked a wary eye at Falk. Doc had the look of a man who, when encountering authority, prefers to keep silent and watch the exit. Falk inclined his head, then took the seat Elissa offered him beside the hearth. His guards arrayed themselves on either side.

Favian sat slightly apart from the rest, facing the door as always and keeping his sword hand free. Although he watched the room carefully, his expression was dazed, as if he were seeing something he could not fully believe.

Falk cleared his throat. There were more people present than he had anticipated, and all of them were looking at him expectantly. He removed his heavy cloak, placing it over his knees. Then, taking Elissa's hands in his own, he began to speak.

"I have been searching for you for months," he said.

Elissa let out a little sigh.

"After I left you, I returned to Castlemar to find my father on his deathbed," he said.

Elissa bit her lip. In spite of the fact that the old man had plotted to kill her and her mother, she could not help but wish he'd lived a little longer. She had few enough family members as it was. If only for a few moments, she would have liked to have seen his face. Had there been any words of forgiveness at the end? A reconciliation? Elissa glanced at her father's face, looking for some sign of inner peace. But his eyes were hooded.

"As his last act, he passed the crown to me," Falk continued. "Once I was crowned, with the complete support of the High Council, the southern duchies pledged their fealty on the spot. We did not have to fight a single battle."

Elissa frowned. "How could they make war on you one day and pledge loyalty the next?"

"A strong king, Elissa, does not hesitate to shed blood. He will march at the head of his troops and give his enemies no quarter. It is better to stand behind a strong king than to take a risk with a weak duke—such as Gavin."

Elissa understood that completely eradicating one's enemies would certainly limit their ability to fight again. Nevertheless, she could not comprehend the practicality of such a strategy when one's enemies might one day be one's friends—and quite a few of them might even be one's relatives. She suspected that in Falk's world there would be many things she would never understand. She nodded for him to continue.

"Once my enemies realized they were in for a real fight, they disbanded. In the end, there was no need for the Khan's troops, or for his backing." Falk took a deep breath. "It was all rather unnecessary."

Falk, as Elissa had realized some time ago, was not the sort of man to apologize. "Rather unnecessary" was probably as close as he could come. Elissa let go of Falk's hand.

"I set out to find you immediately, but by the time I reached the Khan's Citadel, you had gone. The desert storms delayed me even further. I cannot tell you how worried I was. I had to return to Castlemar at that point to attend to affairs of state. By the time I tracked you to Alhamazar, I found I had once again missed you. One of my contacts there informed me that a girl and a donkey had departed only days before. I thank the gods it was not difficult to locate you here. Fortunately, there aren't many young girls who travel with donkeys— What *is* it?"

Maya had begun to giggle. Falk, unaccustomed to being laughed at, could not hide his irritation.

Elissa explained. "You were actually following Maya," she said. "I missed the boat."

"How is that?" he asked. Falk listened closely

as Elissa explained how she had been drugged by the silk merchant in Alhamazar.

"I will do something about that," he said quietly. "But how did you come to Alhamazar?" he asked. "We were to have met on the eastern edge of the forest."

Elissa suddenly realized how little her father knew. He had no concept of what the Khan had planned for her—or for Maya.

Falk's expression grew horrified, then grim, as she described their escape from the Citadel and their harrowing flight through the desert. Elissa's desert journey was news to the rest of the company as well. Apart from Maya, who already knew the tale, they absorbed every word in stunned silence. Favian's hand tightened over the hilt of his sword as Elissa told them of Kreel's attempt to return Maya and her to the Khan as slaves.

"That swine!" Favian cried. Then he reddened as Elissa turned her eyes to him.

Falk cleared his throat. "Go on," he said.

"Well," she said, casting a brief glance at Maya, "the desert people rescued us and brought us to Alhamazar." Best not to explain too much—

yet. "And the rest you already know. Aesha and Favian can speak for themselves."

They could, and did, and when they were finished with their stories there was a hush as everyone collected their thoughts. When all the tales have been told, what is left but silence? An ending, perhaps—or, at the very least, a resolution. Elissa looked at her companions—Aesha, Maya, and Favian—and it suddenly became clear to her what needed to happen next.

"Father . . . ," Elissa began. The word still felt strange on her tongue.

Falk lifted his eyebrows.

"Aesha wants to go back to her people in the Great Circle, which is in the same direction as Castlemar. And Favian"—she glanced at him—"has no home at present." Favian nodded slightly.

Finally Elissa turned to face Maya. "And you'd like to stay with me a little while longer, wouldn't you?" Maya bobbed her head vigorously.

Elissa looked at Falk, faltering. "Do you think—"

Falk replied without hesitation. "My ship lies in the harbor. We can all leave tomorrow." Elissa smiled gratefully. Falk had been both gracious and generous. She would have expected no less from a king.

"Thank you," she said, her eyes shining. She did not know why it was so important that they all leave together, but she knew it was *right*.

"Gangway!" Lily entered the common room with two heavily laden trays balanced in her broad hands. Billy followed close behind with a pitcher of cider.

As Elissa suspected from her temper alone, Lily was an excellent cook. She served up a delicious stew laced with sweet, dark ale over a bed of fragrant saffron rice. Succulent steamed dumplings dotted the edges of each plate like a string of tender pearls. For dessert she had made honey-baked apples in cinnamon butter, topped with crunchy sugared nuts. They washed their repast down with mugs of hot mulled cider. Falk declared it the best meal he had ever eaten, a sentiment enthusiastically shared by the rest of the company, who called for the cook with a round of applause. Lily finally emerged red-faced from the kitchen, carving knife in hand, dimpling with pleasure.

"Now that I've partaken of your excellent cooking," said Falk, eyeing the knife, "I trust I'll be safe for the night."

"Go on with ye!" exclaimed Lily. "I'd never take a carving knife to 'Lissa's dad."

Falk heaved an audible sigh of relief.

"I'd use a cleaver," she said, turning back to the kitchen.

There was a brief, tense silence, which Falk broke by throwing his head back in a sudden, unexpected burst of laughter.

"I could use that woman," he said, wiping his eyes. "Now that Aldric is Regent, I need a new Captain of the Guard." Then he paused, recollecting something. "Ah," he said, "I was so caught up in your tale, I forgot to tell you. The Khan is no longer in power. He has been overthrown by the desert tribes."

Elissa was hardly surprised. After all, she'd made a substantial contribution toward his ouster. But there was another man who worried her as much as, if not more than, the Khan. "What of Kreel?" she asked. "Did they catch him, too?"

Falk hesitated. The details of Kreel's demise

were rather gruesome. "The Blue People do not deal lightly with slave traders, especially those who steal their robes. You will not be troubled by either one of them again," Falk promised.

And, because he was King, he believed it.

After the meal, everyone was hustled upstairs by an adamant Lily, who insisted that there had been enough excitement that day to last them all a hundred years and that, by the gods, they should let the poor girls rest. Nobody dared disagree. Falk patted Elissa's head, a trifle awkwardly, in the common room doorway, wishing her a good night. She bade him good night in return. Maya slipped behind her with a smile and a little wave at the King of Castlemar. Favian clicked his heels and bowed, thoroughly disconcerted but remembering his manners. Aesha said nothing. She made her way slowly and silently up the stairs and down the hallway to her room. It seemed like such a very long way. She was followed by Billy.

"I have something to show you," he said, awkwardly removing his cap. He lifted the latch and pushed open her door. She peered into the room, hesitating.

"It's all right," he said. "Go in."

Next to her bed stood a low table. A lamp had been placed there, illuminating the simple room with its soft glow. The plain armoire, the chair, the rug—all was as it had been that afternoon, except for a small cloth-covered box at the foot of her bed. "Excuse me," Billy mumbled, and went to fetch the box. He placed it on the bed, and when Aesha drew near, he removed the cloth. It was a little wooden cage, inside of which perched a sleeping bird.

"Oh! Oh!" cried Aesha. It was the loudest noise Billy had heard her make. She sounded as if she were in pain. "Let it out!"

"No, marm," Billy said quickly. "It isn't trapped. This is just its little house. See?"

He opened the door to the cage, and the bird yawned and fluffed its feathers. Billy placed his finger inside the cage. The bird eyed it, then lifted one foot and hopped upon it. He withdrew his hand slowly. The bird was a small, nondescript creature, colored a soft gray. Three ruffled feathers rose up comically from the top of its head in an unkempt little circle. It looked precisely as if it had just woken up.

"It's tame," he said, holding the bird out to Aesha. "Take it."

Aesha looked doubtful. The very idea of a cage horrified her. All at once, the bird flew from Billy's finger and landed on Aesha's shoulder. It walked sideways until it found her downy hair. Then it nestled against her neck, cooing. The bird made an enchanting sound, like the tinkling of a tiny fountain. Aesha looked flustered but no longer frightened.

"What kind of bird is this?" she asked.

Billy blushed furiously. He was mangling his cap in his large hands. There was a good chance that at the end of this conversation he would have to replace it.

"It's a Sweetheart Bird," he whispered. "Yer look so sad, and I wanted to give yer something to make yer feel better. And I knew yer wouldn't like a metal thing like a whistle, so I got yer something that could sing, just because maybe yer might miss hearing the singing, as yer lost your voice and all, and a bird isn't heavy." Billy spoke all in a rush. He hadn't thought of what he was going to say, so he simply said whatever came into his head, which even to his own ears sounded like gibberish.

Aesha listened patiently to Billy, then inclined her head toward the little bird. It warbled softly in her ear, and for the first time, she smiled.

"Thank you," she said. "I will take good care of my Sweetheart wherever we go."

Billy stood in Aesha's doorway. He had said everything there was to say, or just about everything, so he merely wished her a good night and walked through the doorway. But he lingered in the hallway facing Aesha's closed door for a few moments before returning to his place by the hearth.

"Just come back to me," he said quietly.

Elissa stood by her window, breathing in the damp night air. Maya, sensing Elissa's desire to be alone, had decided to sleep with Aesha that night. Up until that fateful day in High Crossing when Falk had turned her world on its head, solitude had been Elissa's natural state. And although she loved being surrounded by all her friends, she was finding it difficult to think among them.

They had all laid claim to her somehow, if only to embrace her within the sphere of their affections. And she knew, without ever having to hear any one of them say it, that their feelings for her were genuine. She knew it from their voices, their gestures, the way they looked at her: Maya, Aesha, Billy, the Captain, Doc, Lily—even, perhaps, Favian. And their company had always been welcome. But that single embrace in the courtyard, the one she had looked forward to for so long, left her wanting to be alone.

There was a soft rap at her door. Elissa opened it, expecting to see Lily armed with a hot toddy.

"May I come in?" asked Falk. He had removed his cloak and crown and was dressed in a simple linen shirt and a black doublet and breeches, much like the clothing he had worn the first time she saw him, sitting at Bruno's table.

Elissa nodded dumbly.

He looked around her room briefly. Falk always checked his environs before choosing a seat. There was only one chair, which he took. He gestured toward the bed, so that Elissa might be seated as well. She perched herself on the edge of the mattress. Not too long ago, he had held her hands. Now she clasped them together in her lap.

"It's late, I know," he said. He did not wait for Elissa to demur. "But I wanted to speak to you, in private, before we set sail tomorrow." He let out his breath in a short, dry laugh. "I am afraid we had quite an audience this evening. It wasn't really conducive to talking about . . . personal matters."

Elissa held very still.

Falk looked at her for a long moment before starting to speak again.

"This may not be easy to understand," he said. "But when I came to High Crossing, I was not prepared for you." Falk took a breath. "I had thought about my plans at great length, of course, but I had not considered the effect you would have on me."

Elissa gazed at Falk. She could say nothing.

Falk continued, now speaking softly. "The first time I saw you, in Bruno's hall, you were standing in the doorway. I caught a glimpse of green, just a little flash—like a hummingbird hovering before a flower. And there you were, standing in your mother's dress—the one I gave her. It was like looking at a ghost. And when you looked at me—with her eyes, in her dress—the reality of who you were finally struck me. I could deny your existence no longer. You were hers. And mine. I have never felt so vulnerable in my whole life—so vanquished."

Falk rubbed his eyes. "That's a bad feeling for a prince to have, Elissa. And I think I guarded myself against it for a long time." He reached out to take Elissa's hand, and she gave it to him. His hand was very warm, unexpectedly so. Gently, he wrapped his fingers around hers. "I betrayed your mother's memory, and her love," he said. "I will never do that again. From now on, I will be Father first, King second."

When Falk rose, it was to take Elissa in his arms once again. This time he did not smell of armor but of wool and horses—the comforting scents of a father. He held her for a long time while she rested quietly against him. Finally she stirred.

"Father," she said. "May I ask a favor?"

Falk brushed his hand over the top of her head, smiling. "Anything," he said. "Just ask and it is yours."

"May I have a camel?"

The Wrong Direction

Castlemar's royal galleon lay in the harbor, ready to set sail with six new passengers aboard. The animals were loaded first, an event that produced equal parts hilarity and anxiety on the part of the crew.

"Weirdest horse I ever did see!" one of the sailors cried. "Sure hope it can swim!"

Ralph was unfazed by the rocking boat, the waves, the huge expanse of water. "Oh, Gerty," he cried as they walked over the boarding ramp. "Our first cruise together!"

Gertrude swished her tail as she put a cautious hoof on the plank. "I'm already seasick," she said.

The crew of the *Swamp Maiden,* along with the intrepid Lily, had all assembled in the kitchen to send their guests off with hot cider and baskets of warm rolls. Elissa had not bid farewell to many people in her life, and so it pained her to say goodbye. But there was one person who was not there. While the others were preparing to make the short, damp journey to Gravesport's wharves, Elissa climbed the narrow stairway to bid the Captain a fond farewell.

"I'll miss that brew of yours, lass," said the Captain.

"Don't worry, I've left Doc the recipe," said Elissa. Doc, who had followed her up the stairs with the Captain's breakfast, smiled contentedly. Elissa had left him with several "recipes," including one that would prevent seasickness. He intended to make good use of them all.

"Ah, sorry I couldn't come down to meet your father. Doc tells me he's quite a man," the Captain said. Doc winked conspiratorially at Elissa. Apparently Doc had not yet conveyed a vital piece of information to the Captain about Elissa's father.

Elissa smiled. "He is," she said. She patted the Captain on the shoulder, wishing him a rapid recovery. Then she embraced Doc and said goodbye.

Doc corrected her. "Until we meet again," he said. "There are no goodbyes in this world."

Elissa pondered that statement. She certainly hoped that what he said was true. Although her voyage aboard the *Swamp Maiden* had been fraught with uncertainty, and even dangers, she hated to think that she would never see that ungainly vessel again, or its crew. "Until we meet again," she said.

Elissa made her way to the pier in an easier frame of mind. Somehow she knew Doc was right. People like Doc and Cappy and Billy don't simply disappear from one's life. They were too . . . important. Eventually they were bound to cross paths again.

Aesha, Favian, Maya, and Falk all stood in a tight knot on the pier as Falk's men prepared the galleon for departure. The wind was picking up, batting at their hair and coloring their cheeks, but they all looked happy at the prospect of a voyage. Falk, in an effort at camaraderie, had removed his crown for the occasion. Elissa took her place beside him.

Lily grasped Elissa by the shoulders. "Be safe,"

she said. She patted Aesha softly on her arms, saying nothing.

When she caught Favian's eye, she muttered a rueful "Sorry about that thing with the knife."

Favian nodded graciously. "It happens all the time," he said. Then Lily put her strong arms around Maya, lifting her right off the ground to give her a great bear hug.

When she finally addressed Falk, she looked him straight in the eye. "You take good care of my girls," she said. It was not a request.

Falk thoughtfully replied that he intended to, as indeed he did.

Billy gave Favian his hand, sincerely wishing him good speed and a safe journey. He patted Maya fondly on the head, and even though Elissa was now a princess, he put a brotherly arm around her. "Don't be keeping company with any of them fancy sailors," he said, cocking his head toward the galleon. "Yer can't trust 'em."

But when he came to Aesha, he stood frozen before her, trying to think of something significant to say. He couldn't, so he just stood there, looking at her mournfully while she regarded him with her ever-changing eyes. The little bird peeked out from behind her hair and trilled softly.

Aesha extended her long, long arm and laid a pale hand lightly on Billy's shoulder. "I will remember you," she said.

Billy gazed at her as she walked down the pier. Being remembered wasn't enough for him. He decided that if she did not return to him, he would come for her—wherever she might be. He watched steadfastly as she boarded the galleon under the flag of the House of Castlemar. The sailors untied the moorings and shoved off. Then they scrambled up the rigging and unfurled the sails.

And the royal galleon *Galantha* spread her lovely white wings and flew away.

Elissa leaned against the side of Falk's galleon as she creaked and heaved her way north to Castlemar, her sails filled with a warm southerly wind. Elissa's eyes skimmed across the endless marching swells of the waves like a bird looking for a place to land. *The sea is a vast place,* she thought, *not unlike the desert.* She gazed at the distant eastern horizon. It was irresistible, that steady gray line. If you watched it long enough, it disappeared into the sky—almost like watching the earth itself vanish. She shivered slightly in the sea breeze and turned to face the deck, where Favian was talking with Lord Falk, now King Falk. Her father. It was odd, but once she had uttered the simple word "Father," it was as if she had found a secret password. With it, she had opened the doors to their hearts. Elissa traced the features of her father's face with her eyes, seeking familiarity. It was a good feeling, that connection, though she did not yet know what it entailed for the future. She had never been a daughter before.

At present, Falk was examining something with the pinpoint concentration of a hawk. He lifted it, and Elissa saw that it was the black cylinder that had done such harm to the Captain. Then he lowered it again. With their dark, lean faces intently bent over the weapon, Elissa thought Falk and Favian resembled nothing more than father and son. No doubt they were discussing battle strategies, tactics, war. If Doc were here, he would say, in his philosophical fashion, that this was the way of men. Elissa didn't know if her father would understand the horror she felt at such "ways." Perhaps, being a king, he was just as philosophical as Doc. She wondered if Favian would share that perspective once he had regained his Leonne.

Favian had not said much to her since Falk had entered the courtyard, but she could tell that his attitude toward her had shifted. Gone was all semblance of arrogance. He now treated her with utter deference. Such was the power of a title. Elissa shook her head. She was the same person— just Elissa. She sighed. In a way, she was glad she had not told him about her Gift. For a moment, in the courtyard, she had felt an affinity with him. They had both lived their lives with a secret, and to share it would have been a boon to them both. But in all likelihood, Favian would never be able to judge her according to her merits alone. His was a world dominated by rank and title. Favian, she believed, could only see her as a commoner or as nobility. For some reason, that knowledge disappointed her immeasurably.

Elissa shifted her gaze to the bow, where Maya and Aesha stood side by side. Maya looked jubilant; her face, glistening with salt spray, was fixed adoringly on the sea. The Water Girl was happy, so close to her element. So was Aesha. She stood tall and straight. The constant blowing of the wind over the chilly seas had an invigorating effect on her. Though still pale, she had shed some of her strange translucence. Battered by the full force of the wind, Aesha seemed to gain strength and substance. She soared upon the breeze, lifted into its embrace. She was beautiful.

To replace the Windsinger's worn rags, Maya had wrapped Elissa's length of silk artfully around her. The majority of the length she had pleated and tucked into Aesha's waistband, leaving the remainder to cross over her bodice and hang over one shoulder. Now the silk fluttered about the Windsinger's slender body, just like the wings of the little bird that kept warbling, "I love you, I love you," into Aesha's ear. Someday Elissa would translate the little bird's message, if Aesha hadn't discovered it for herself already.

Elissa turned once again to face the boundless sea. At last she was going to Castlemar, to her real home. And among Falk's family, however distant and quarrelsome they might be, she would finally find her place. Everything was going to work out just fine.

Why, then, did she keep looking out at the distant horizon? What was there? She narrowed her eyes toward the place where the sea disappeared into the sky, to where the earth ended. There was no reason for this feeling, she told herself, this feeling that she was still looking for something. She had found what she was seeking— her father, his love, her home. What could possibly be amiss?

The waves slapping steadily against the side of the ship seemed to beat in time to their own mysterious song, a whispered cadence that only the creatures of the sea could understand: it was the secret of the far horizon. Try as she might, Elissa could not quite make out the words. Closing her eyes, she leaned against the side of the rocking ship and listened.

The end of the world is near, whispered the waves.

"I wonder what's in here," said Maya.

After supper, which they took with Falk in his quarters, Maya and Elissa retired to the adjoining stateroom. The room was sumptuous, boasting carved maple furnishings, wine velvet drapes, and an immense bed with fluffy pillows. Elissa thought that nothing could have been more unlike her swinging hammock on the *Swamp Maiden*'s ramshackle second deck.

Elissa sat on the edge of the bed, brushing her hair, while Maya busily inspected the room for hidden treasure.

"Gowns!" Maya cried, sticking her head out of an immense armoire. She pulled out a velvet-trimmed brocade dress. "It's too big for me," she said. "But I think it will fit you."

Elissa nodded, but said nothing while Maya continued to open doors and rummage through chests.

"What's the matter?" asked Maya. She was holding a mirror inlaid with mother-of-pearl. "Aren't you happy?"

"Of course I am!" said Elissa.

Maya made her way to the bed and hopped onto the satin coverlet, next to Elissa. She held the mirror in front of Elissa's face. "No, you're not," she said. "Look!"

Elissa regarded her own face. Except for glimpses of her image caught in pools of water and the occasional shiny metal plate, she'd never seen a true reflection of her own features before—certainly not with such clarity. Her face wasn't quite as she remembered. She had the same high forehead, the same chin. But her cheeks looked less plump, and the green eyes looking gravely back at her, with a mixture of apprehension and doubt, seemed older.

"No," said Elissa. "I *am* happy. But I keep feeling that something is wrong and I can't put my finger on it."

"Is it us?" asked Maya. "Would you rather be alone with your father?"

Elissa pushed the mirror away. "Oh dear," she said. "Not at all. In fact, having everybody here with me is the only thing that feels right."

"Then what's the problem?" asked Maya. She folded her hands, preparing to listen.

Elissa looked into Maya's trusting brown eyes. There was so much she hadn't told her—about the men in the jungle and what she had almost done to them, about the firesticks, about Favian. She knew she would have to share all of that, but not tonight. Because even though her adventures aboard the *Swamp Maiden* still remained to be told, there was something else she needed to discuss with Maya—something only her dear friend would understand.

"I keep thinking I am supposed to do something," said Elissa. "Remember what Om Chai said? She said I had to find something."

"She said to find *them*," corrected Maya. She frowned. "Maybe she meant *us*."

Suddenly it all clicked into place. "Yes!" said Elissa triumphantly. "That's it! I had found *you* already. But I needed to find Favian and Aesha, too. So that's four of us."

"But Om Chai said, '*Three* are found, yet *two* remain,' " said Maya. "That's five in all." She held up her hand and ticked off her fingers. "There's Favian and Aesha. Then there's you and me. So who is the fifth? Your father?"

"Maybe," said Elissa doubtfully. "But I don't think so. He's not . . . like us." Elissa didn't know if she should tell Maya about Favian's Gift. It was plainly a secret he had kept carefully guarded.

"I know," said Maya seriously. "He's a king." The corners of her mouth started to twitch.

Elissa hit Maya with a pillow. "Silly girl," she said.

Maya tucked the pillow under her head. "Let's figure it out tomorrow," she said, yawning. "After all, the problem will still be here in the morning, and so will we. Right now I'm sleepy." Then, before Elissa's very eyes, Maya fell fast asleep.

Elissa blew out the candle, amazed at Maya's ability to fall unconscious at the drop of a hat. She stretched herself out on the bed, ordering herself to sleep. But unlike Maya, she couldn't simply curl up, close her eyes, and forget the world. And that night, the world stayed very much with her. As soon as she had chased one question from her mind, another took its place. Who was the fifth person? The prophecy was too obscure for her to understand—Maya certainly had more of a grasp on it than she did—but clearly there was someone else involved. What was she supposed to do once she found him . . . or her? And what did Om Chai mean by "The end of the world is near"? As she pondered Om Chai's prophecy, the feeling of foreboding she'd had earlier intensified. Finally she could stand it no longer. Elissa rose, threw on her cloak, and walked out onto the main deck, where she stood looking out over the dark waters. She felt a small flutter by her ear.

"Moth," she whispered, "tell me what it all means."

But the moth said nothing, or at least nothing she could hear over the slap of the waves. She brushed her hair away from her ear and tilted her head, focusing all her attention.

She thought she heard the tiny voice say, "Back."

Go back? Come back? Where?

The deck creaked behind her, making her jump.

"Oh, I am sorry. I didn't mean to startle you," said Favian. He stood beside her in stiff-backed silence, almost at attention.

Elissa lifted her face to the night sky, holding very still. But it was no use. The little flutter was gone.

Favian hadn't moved; he was clearly waiting for her to speak. "The stars are bright tonight," she said, in order to say something.

"The eyes of the gods," said Favian formally. "They are watching over us."

Elissa thought for a moment. "They don't look like eyes," she said. "They look more like distant fires."

Favian relaxed a bit. He turned in the darkness and held out his palms to her. "As a matter of fact, they are."

She looked at his hands. "You can feel the stars, even at such a distance," she marveled. She looked into Favian's dark eyes. They were so much alike—if only he would treat her as an equal.

Favian cleared his throat. He had something to say. "Princess . . . ," he began.

Elissa drew away from him. Having Favian put her above him was even worse than treating her like a simple peasant. At least she actually *was* a peasant—if not a simple one. And tonight these courtly pretensions of his were more than she could bear. She turned and started to say good night, but Favian interrupted her.

"Elissa," he said.

His voice was soft, but there was something in his tone that made Elissa halt.

"I hope I have not offended you," he said.

"You have not," she said, but she did not look at him.

Favian breathed deeply and took the plunge. "I realize that my behavior toward you has been truly disgraceful," he said. "This is a result of my upbringing, which does not excuse it, nor does it make my conduct acceptable. You saved my life and expected nothing in return. You also saved Aesha from a fate worse than death, simply because her plight touched your heart. Your courage, generosity, and honesty are what make you the person you are. Peasant or princess, it doesn't matter, for you need nothing more than the stars above you to be crowned in glory."

Elissa stood before Favian, at a loss for words. She could feel her heart beating.

Favian unsheathed his sword and, kneeling, placed it at her feet. "My sword is at your disposal, Elissa. As is my loyalty." In all his life, Favian had never bowed his head in apology. He bowed it now and waited.

Looking down at Favian, who had bowed his head not in respect for her rank but in simple humility, Elissa suddenly felt like crying. She extended her hand and gave him a brief, light touch on the shoulder. Favian raised his eyes and looked at her expectantly. Now it was her turn to be humble.

"Thank you," she said. "We may have need of your sword."

"Upon my honor, no one will harm you or yours while I live." He pronounced each word with all the intensity his soul could muster. And this time, knowing his intentions were pure, Elissa could not deny him his courtly flourish, his aristocratic gesture. She left his honor and his pride intact. The ship creaked, rocking gently as it cut its way through the waves that ran swiftly before the southerly winds, and the stars shone bright above them. When Favian rose and took Elissa by the hand, she did not withdraw it.

"And may my life be very long," he said, "so that I will always be here to defend you."

Elissa's smile came straight from her heart.

"Peace?" said Favian.

"Peace," replied Elissa.

After Favian had gone below, Elissa held her hand up against the sky. It seemed to glow faintly, but that may have been starlight.

Will wonders never cease, she thought. Underneath all that bravado, Favian was a real person. What was more, he was a *good* person. She had been very wrong about him, but maybe the conflict between them had served a purpose. Now they *had* to get to know one another. And, Elissa had to admit, having a loyal friend—especially one who knew something about weaponry—was a comfort to her. Because something was terribly wrong.

The feeling that she was being watched was so strong that she felt compelled to turn to see what lurked behind her. But there was only the faint line of the horizon. It tugged at her, pulling her eyes toward it. She didn't know what she was looking for, only that she needed to find *something* that would identify the source of her discomfort. She knew it was out there somewhere. But it seemed that the more she gazed, the less that narrow edge served to separate the dark sea from the even darker firmament above it. Just as she had that afternoon, Elissa focused on the place where one dark mass blended into the other until there was no distinguishing between sea and sky. Awareness drifted away.

Then, and only then, when the boundaries of her mind were as insubstantial as the separation between heaven and earth, did the full realization come to her.

They were headed in the wrong direction.

Erica Verrillo is a world traveler who has studied and worked in a variety of fields, including classical music, Latin American history, linguistics, folk dance, anthropology, refugee aid, and speech communication. She has been a teacher of languages, public speaking, linguistics, and music. She lives in Massachusetts with her two children.